FROM CEMETERY TO SEMINARY

V.J. Mathews
Vanniyamparambil

FROM CEMETERY
TO
SEMINARY
Novel

(English Version of Malayalam novel "Tharangam" Published in

2017 by Kerala Sahithya Mandalam)

Author

This is a work of fiction. Any resemblances to persons living or dead as to actual incident are purely coincidental. The war details are also imaginary

When you turn the pages

<u>Editor's Note</u>

This Novel is written in the backdrop of the Socio– economic situation that prevailed in the mid twentieth century in Kerala, a Southern State of India. Caste System was still prevalent in the Society at that time. Caste and Colour were the fundamental determining factors of one's Social status. Besides, financial status also was a deciding factor.

Ouseph and Martin, though Christians by faith, represented two different Social Status. Ouseph, who belonged to the lower caste and black in colour, was looked down by everyone including the Parish Priest who is supposed to be the representative of Jesus who taught that everyone is a child of God. Martin, on the other hand, belonged to the upper class, though financially poor.

The Novel narrates the revolutionary friendship between Martin and Ouseph and later unfolds their extraordinary success in life.

The Novelist exposes his protest against the existing system that prevailed in society and in religion. In the selection of Ouseph, who was the son of a gravedigger, to the Seminary in Vatican, his close association with Holy Father the Pope are to be seen in this perspective. Again, the author makes Catherine, an Italian Duchess, to fall in love with Ouseph which ended up in their happy married life is a slap on the face of Indian hypocracy. While Indian Society degrade the low caste people, Europeans treat everyone with human dignity.

The Novelist makes use of every opportunity to express his views on Religious Values including God. He never leaves a chance to criticize the shortcomings of Christianity, though, at the same time depicts exemplary characters among whom we can see Pope, Bishops and priests.

Though we may not be able to endorse all his ideas on religion and religious values, we will be attracted to many of his views when we read the novel with an open mind.

Davis Madavana

FROM CEMETRY TO SEMINARY

CHAPTER : ONE

FOUNDATION OF A LEGEND

Marso International Private Limited' was one of the leading and well reputed Exporting Companies in Cochin, Kerala in 1970's. The Company was widely known by its trade name 'Marso'

``Marso' was functioning in a two storied building of its own at Bristow road Willington Island Cochin, very near to Ernakulam Wharf. They had a freezing plant at Kannamaly, and that was the biggest one in Cochin. Their main business was exporting fresh vegetable and other perishable food stuff to Gulf sector.

Head office of the Company was in Dubai. Mr. Ransisy, an Italian was the Chief Executive. Later his niece Mrs. Catherine Ouso became the Chief Executive. The operations of Cochin Office was controlled and managed by Mr. Martin Manassery, Director of the Company. He was a Keralite, from Mundalam, Pala.

Mr. Ouso, the husband of Mrs. Catherine also was a Keralite and from Pala. His earlier name was Ouseph. The full name was

Palliparambil Pathrose Ouseph; officially P.P. Ouseph, later became Ouso.

This is the history of the world renowned multicrore exporting and trading company 'Marso International Private Limited.' This is also the story of two different personalities, Martin and Ouseph.

Martin and Ouseph were very thick friends from their boyhood days. They studied together in the same school, same class; and seated side by side . However, there were vast differences in their complexions, culture, social status and dignity.

Martin, though he was financially poor, was blue blooded, and belonged to an ancient Catholic family named 'Manassery'. His grand father John Manassery was a wholesale grain merchant at Alleppy. Martin had a charming personality with curly hair and fair complexion.

 Ouseph also was Catholic but belonged to a lower caste 'Pulaya Convert' a socially backward community. His complexion was dark and his face had a rough look. His father Pathrose was a grave digger in the cemetry of 'Mundalam' Catholic Church.

Both had one in common. That was poverty and both were starving for food during their school days. This made Martin and Ouseph thick friends.

'Pulaya' community was considered to be backward and very inferior in the society. They were deprived of equality and justice even in Churches. Hindu orthodox community maintained untouchability with Pulaya caste. Further, the grave digging was considered to be the most menial job one can imagine. Being the son of a grave digger, Ouseph was deprived of all privileges at School. However the caste difference did not hinder the intimacy and friendship amongMartin and Ouseph.

Prior to 1950's, Manassery family was one of the richest Christian families in Kerala.

There was a big tragedy which made Manassery family to plunge into poverty.

Martin's grand father, John Manassery, had the business of importing rice from Burma (present Myanmar) by ship and distributing throughout the coastal towns of Kerala, by country crafts and boats. It was a very big business at that time. John Manassery had owned five motor boats and twelve large country crafts. Loaded country crafts were towed by the boats. He had fifty headload workers and ten boat workers as his permanent employees. He had three big godowns to store imported rice, and a big wholesale shop at Alleppy market, near Mullackal Canal.

`All lost with in no time, like a thunder strike. `A ship load of consignment of rice was reported to be lost in the sea. There were three versions on the mishap. One was that the merchant ship was looted by the pirates. The second was that the ship loaded with thousand tons of rice sunk in mid sea due to storm. The third version was that John Manassery was cheated by the Burmese trader. He had submitted a false " Bill of Lading" to the bank and withdrawn the entire money sent by John but not shipped the consignment.

Whatever be the case, John Manassery became bankrupt and he had to sell his entire property, godowns, shop and even his house to clear the debt with the bank. He became a 'Pauper'.

John could not withstand the strain and stress when he became no one in the society. The merchant committed suicide by hanging himself inside his godown.

When everything was lost, his only son Joseph fled from his home town Alleppy, came to Pala, purchased a small two room house with thirty cents of land at Mundalan Village, four kilometers away from Pala town and started living there with his wife Eliamma and two sons Michael and Martin. His collegemate Vasudevan Varrier of Mundalam native, helped him to settle down. He also helped him to start Tapioca trading (colloquially called 'Kappa') for his lively hood. Boiled Kappa and Mathy curry (Sardine fish) was widely accepted and used by poor natives as their main food in those days. Though rice was the main food of Keralites, it was very dear and short in the market, in those days (1950')

The unexpected and sudden demise of his friend Vasudevan varrier put Joseph into misery and helplessness.

Joseph did not have sufficient capital to run the 'Kappa trading' for long. He started to cultivate Kappa in a leased land. One day Joseph was digging in his plantation with a spade to manure. It was drizzling then. He did not bother. He continued to dig throughout the day in rain. Next day he was hospitalized due to high fever. It became very serious and pneumonia infected his lungs. On the fourth day he died.

It was a great tragedy for Manassery family. They plunged into utter poverty. At that time Martin was studying in seventh standard and Michael was in tenth. In those days, in the late 1950's the cost of one kilo rice was only fifty paise. Cost of one kilo kappa was only ten paise. Eliamma, mother of Michael and Martin found it difficult to make ten paisa to buy a kilo of kappa to feed her children.

Knowing their pathetic situation their neighbour Sarada teacher, widow of Vasudevan Varrier helped Manassery family by giving them the required kappa on credit. Sarada teacher had a daughter Radha, who was studying in fifth class in a Convent School.

Most of the days Michael and Martin were going to school without their lunch pack. Starving during lunch time became a practice for them.

Ouseph, though he was son of a grave digger and from a backward community, never missed his lunch. He went to school always with his lunch pack. He carried steamcooked kappa and 'chilly chutney' in his tiffin box. n those days students used to take only rice for their lunch. Ouseph did not have any delicacy to take kappa for his lunch.

He was well accustomed and tamed in receiving insult and abuses from the society, since he belonged to an untouchable backward caste.

But for Michael and Martin, taking boiled kappa for their lunch to school was a shame as they belonged to Manassery family, though poor. Once they were very rich and aristocratic. They were grandchildren of a great rice whole sale merchant of Alleppy market, Joseph Manassery.

One day, it was lunch break time in the school. Martin did not have anything to eat. He continued to sit in his seat and started doing his home work.

Students who brought their lunch packs opened their tiffin boxes and started to eat. That was the practice. They were not provided with separate dining place in the School. Everybody had to have their lunch in their respective class rooms.

Class room was filled with the odour of food. The aroma infected pain in Martin's jaws and saliva flooded in his month. Burning sensation upsurged from his stomach. He felt the intestine was burning inside the stomach. His eyes were moistened and tears rolled down through his cheeks. Tear drops fell on his note book and the ink smudged in the sheets.

Michael borrowed forty paisa from his friend and went to a nearby hotel. He ate two Dosas there itself and bought two Dosa, wrapped in a paper, ran to Martin's class room and gave it to his younger brother.

Dosa is a type of pancake, widely ate in south India at break fast. It is made from fermented rice and black gram batter, get it fried in pan. Usually Dosa is eaten along with coconut chutney.

When Martin opened the Dosa packet, Ouseph, who was sitting by his side   eating boiled kappa, looked at Dosa with widened eyes and said." I have forgotten when I ate Dosa last. May be years back. Kappa is my only food. All the three times a day only kappa. If you give me half Dosa, in return, I will give you a big piece of Banana Kappa."

 Ouseph had no   delicacy in putting up requests to any one. The fate of his caste was that they had to beg even for their rights.

"Banana Kappa.? What is that? I never heard of such a Kappa" Martin said with astonishment.

"Banana Kappa is a special breed. This variety is not   available anywhere in Kerala. 'Koyikal' family had imported its stumps from

Brazil and planted it. It is very very tasty. It is as good as boiled banana. Do you want a try? Give me half of Dosa, I will give you one big piece of boiled Banana Kappa. It is very delicious than your Dosa.".

"How did you get this Kappa? Did 'Koikal' family people give it to you?" Martin asked.

"Koikal family people are the most misers in the world. They won't give anything to anyone. So I stole it at night from their Kappa grove." Ouseph said openly.

"You mean you stole it?"

"Christ said in Bible to give to who ever ask. Christ never said what to do if not given.   That means you can steel. So I stole. I also have to survive in this world.

Martin gave half portion of a Dosa to Ouseph against one big piece of Banana Kappa.

What Ouseph said was true. The boiled Banana Kappa was delicious and Martin liked it.

"Dosa would melt away before it reaches the stomach, though tasty. Kappa will quench the hunger, and it will sustain in the bowels for longer time. We can survive the whole day with two three pieces of Kapa." Ouseph said and ate the Dosa enjoying it.

The exchange of Dosa and Kappa was the first business transaction Martin and Ouseph had done while they were students. That became the foundation of their future joint venture of multi crore export business "Marso International Pvt.Ltd"

CHAPTER TWO

BORN IN FIRE

"Meenachil River" flows through the heart of 'Pala' Taluk in Kottayam District. The water of the river was very clean and even drinkable in early days. The river makes the whole of Pala a paradise in the valley of Eastern Ghats.

'Manassery' house was situated in "Mundalam' Village, about four Kilo meters east to Pala town, by the west bank of Meenachil river. Martin's house was a small tile roofed building and bricks as wall, with two rooms and a portico. Earlier that building was used as a store by a planter from whom Joseph Manassery, father of Michael and Martin bought with the help of his friend Chelattu Vasudevan varier. Both studied together in Government College, Vaikom.

Joseph constructed two leans on both sides of the house, one shed was used as kitchen and the other was used by Michael and Martin as their living room.

A country fence with yellow bamboo was erected around the enclosure of thirty cents of land, and the enclosure was fully utilized for the cultivation of Tapioca (Kappa) a very popular and common agriculture in that region.

Meenachil river was flowing very near to the house. There was a rubble paved bathing ghat very near to Manassery house, later known to be 'Manassery Kadav'. On the other bank, opposite to " Manassery Kadav", there was another bathing ghat known as "Pulaya Kadav", meaning the ghat used by the Pulaya community. House of Ouseph, a thatched hut was situated very near to the 'Pulayakadav", which was back side of Mundalam Catholic Church. The Church Cemetery was situated within the compound wall and that was very near to Ouseph's house.

Ouseph lost his mother when he was seven years old, during a flood time. Meenachil river was then over flowing. It was said that she had slipped and fell in the high current of flood water. Her body was found a few kilometres down stream stuck in bamboo grove. There was another saying that the lady had committed suicide by jumping in to the flood water. She was fed up living with Pathrose, the grave digger who was a drunkard. When drunk, Pathrose was a devil and he was drinking all the time.

Many including the Parish priests had tried several times to stop his drinking habit by advice and counselling.

 "My job is a nasty one. Re opening used grave to bury new corpse is really a horrible work. Without half a bottle of arrack (liquor) in the stomach and its spirit in veins, no one would be able to bear the stinking smell." That was his justification for drinking.

From the very child hood Ouseph had to live on his own. He had to cook for his father too. Not much of a cooking though: boiling of 'kappa' and preparing of pungent chilly chutney. Ouseph was very smart in making pungent chilly chutney.

The Parishioners of Mundalam Church were not that liberal in giving kappa to the grave digger and his son free. If not given when asked, Ouseph used to sneak into the tapioca grove at night and steel whatever kappa he wanted. What he wanted was just three or four kilos of kappa for a day. Rice was then a luxury food for him. and buying raw rice was far beyond his capacity. Cost of raw rice was fifty paisa per kilo at that time. Wages for digging a grave was two rupees. And that was not sufficient for Pathrose to drink toddy and arrak.

Though Ouseph belonged to a lower caste and lived in utter poverty he was a brilliant student in the school, always scoring high marks in all subjects.

However, there was a discrimination between higher and lower caste students. Pulaya students were not allowed to sit in the front rows; they were allotted with back seats in the class. Being the tallest student, Martin also was always allotted back seat and he was sitting near Ouseph in all the classes from 5th to 10th.

Having a morning swim in Meenachil River was a daily routine of Martin and Ouseph. The width of the river at Mundalam area was about two hundred and fifty meters. Depth of water was about three meters. The current was very low except in Monsoon. In Monsoon season river would become wild and the current would be fierce.

But for Ouseph all seasons were alike. He used to swim across the river even in severe floods. Swimming between the two ghats was a pleasure for him. It was for him a bravery act in flood time. If anyone asked, why he was not afraid of swimming in high current, his reply would be "The spirit of my mother is in that current, and so, she would protect me"

Sarada teacher, wife of late Vadudevan Varier , the immediate neighbour of Manassery house, was very helpful to Eliamma and her children Michael and Martin. She was middle aged and rich. She owned a Tapioca plantation of eight acres, later converted it as a Rubber Plantation.   Eliamma used to send her sons to buy kappa on credit but seldom paid, and Sarada teacher did not have any complaint.

Sarada teacher used to send her only daughter Radha along with Martin every day to river ghats for morning bath.

"Martin, son, please take care of child Radha. She should not go to the deep water. Let her take bath standing on the ghat steps. Please take extra care on the child, your sister." Sarada teacher used to give caution whenever Radha went with Martin to ghats.

When Martin and Radha would appear at Manassery ghats, Ouseph who was waiting for them at the other bank, 'Pulaya kadav', would jump into river and swim towards them . When reaches west bank, he would sit on the ghats steps   and talk to them. Sometimes Ouseph would perform many hydromantic tricks in the water to entertain Radha. Lifting both legs vertically up in the air while the rest of the body from the chest below the water level was one of his main items.

Swim with one hand, holding his cloth in the other hand above water

was another item. Floating on the water with hands and legs spread

out was yet another number.

He could swim back stroke at the same speed as that of free style. He

was an expert in under water diving too. Holding his breath up to the

count of two hundred under water was another astonishing

performance.

Earlier, Radha was very reluctant to mingle with the lower caste black

youth. Later, when she came to know about his extraordinary talents

and gifted brilliance in studies she started to admire him.

Years has passed on fast. Martin and Ouseph reached 9th class and

Radha at seventh.

One day early in the morning, Martin and Radha were at the bathing

ghats getting ready for bath as usual. Ouseph reached from the other

bank swimming. He was stark naked. His bathing towel was around his

neck.

"Hay, look Marty brother, that blacky lad is naked." Radha covered her face with both her palms and said aloud in a shocking voice. However she was peeping through her finger gaps.

Martin looked at Ouseph who was swimming fast towards them. He was about to reach the bank. Martin thought Ouseph would come out of water and climb the steps of ghats nude. But, Ouseph made a howling voice and turned to return. He made a mighty leap to dive under the water, exposing his pitch dark skinned buttock above the water. It was a great fun for Martin and Radha. Martin laughed aloud. Radha could not resist laughing. She also hauled along with Martin joyously.

Ouseph swam back again towards them. At that time he had his towel fastened around his waist. He came out of water and sat on the steps panting.

Radha was taking bath by dipping her body in the water, by standing on a step, where water was only up to her upper abdomen. She dipped her head in the water and raised. Her curly hair which was on her chest through the shoulders, floated away and her bare chest became visible. The budding breasts were noticeable.

Ouseph had seen it and he said in a serious tone. "Sister, Radha, please don't get offended if I give you a bit of advice; as your brother. I think it is my duty and right to tell you this. In fact, your mother should have told you this."

"What is that?" Radha demanded and Martin looked at Ouseph eagerly.

"Radha, you are not a child anymore. You are becoming a girl. Girls should not expose their chest when growing. And one more thing. You may please stop taking bath in ghats with boys."

Radha felt utter shame and had lost her honour. She felt as if she was fully naked and exposed. She never had such a diffidence feeling in her whole life. Her eyes became wet and her face became pale. She came out of water in a hurry and climbed up the steps quickly . She dressed up swiftly even without drying her head and body. She ran out of the ghats, as if she was frightened to death.

"You stupid… you should not have talked to her in that manner." Martin said   in an arrogant tone.

"I said a fact. That's all. You need not bother about it. " Ouseph said very casually.

"Any way, I think it is not a decent talk. It was not nice."

"Truths won't be nice sometimes."

"What right do you have to advise her like that?"

"I do not have any right..agreed. But Martin, we are not saints. We are in our adolescence. Adolescents are inquisitive always. She is a child in her heart. But her body is growing. Suppose in case either of us happened to touch her bud, you know what will happen? The childlike innocence in her will be lost forever. She would become a woman. An immature woman. Immature women get spoiled quickly. I don't want that happen to her." Ouseph said authoritatively.

"You talk like a wise man." There was a surprise in Martin's voice.

"I am not a wise man. But, I know the world better than you. I was born in fire and never get fade in sun".

Thereafter, Radha never went with Martin to bathing ghats. Martin never called her either.

CHAPTER 3

SCHOOL DAYS

It was a great surprise to every one when Michael who was always silent and aloof stood "First in State" in the SSLC examination held in 1956. He was also awarded with Gold Medal by Education Ministry for his exemplary performance.

Everybody expected that he would go for higher studies. But he preferred to seek an employment. There was an advertisement in News Papers inviting application from graduates for apprenticeship in a Shipping Company at Cochin. Though not a graduate, he sent an application without any expectation. He had enclosed the newspaper cutting which contained the report of his award along with the application. Though he never expected even an interview card, what he received was an appointment order, as an 'Export Executive Trainee' with a monthly stipend of four hundred rupees per month. It was a very high salary in those days.

There was an apprehension in Eliamma's mind to send Michael to Cochin, where he has to live alone. Till then, he never lived alone any where other than at his house   . Sarada teacher had offered to go along with Michael to Cochin. She had her relatives living there, she said. But Michael refused .

"I told you before Amma,   I hate that lady." He told Eliamma personally.

"But why my son? She is a nice person and very helpful to us" Eliamma argued.

 Michael did not explain further. She understood that there was a secret hehind his irritation to Sarada,   But could not guess what it was.

Michael went alone to Cochin, and joined in 'Govardhan Shipping Company' as an executive trainee. Very quickly he could familiarise with the jobs assigned to him. His job was to supervise the loading and unloading of consignments in wharf where huge ships were anchored. Slowly he became familiar with city life and gradually he became a city man.

Four hundred rupees per month was a big money for Michael. Two hundred rupees was just sufficient enough for a thrifty man like him to live for a month. One square meal at hotel was costing fifty paise only. For breakfast, pancakes like dosa or appam cost only ten paisa.

Snacks like vada, bonda, cutlet etc were costing five to ten paisa either. Ten paisa for a cup of tea.

Cost of living was very low in those days . Money value also was very low. Dollar value was twenty seven rupees and one sovereign of gold was costing only seventy rupees.

Michael was staying at Fort Cochin near 'Amman coil Temple' in an Advocate's double storied house named ''Mana' as a 'paying guest', by paying three rupees per month. His travel expenses by boat from Fort Cochin to Willigndon Island, where he was working, was only fifty paise per day to and fro. Somehow, he could manage to save two hundred rupees a month to send to his mother and brother living at Mundalam, Pala.

It was a great relief for Eliamma and Martin. They were relieved from the tight grip of poverty. Out of two hundred rupees received from Michael, Eliamma could save some money. She could pay off all her debts. With the help of her neighbour Sarada teacher, Eliamma started a poultry farm in a small way with fifty chicks. Within a year her poultry had grown to a farm with four hundred chicks. The main chicken feed was waste tapioca collected from tapiocagardens and got it pulverised in machine. Eliamma was getting waste tapioca free of cost from farms. Martin used to collect them in gunny bags and carried by head load. Chicken liked pulverised tapioca granules and it was available in plenty. Eliamma was getting about two hundred and fifty eggs per day. Cost of one egg was ten paisa. There was good demand for eggs.

Next year Michael came on leave with lot of gifts and presents to his mother and brother. When heard, Sarada teacher was a regular visitor to Manassery house, Michael got annoyed.

"I don't like that lady coming here." He got irritated.

"Don't be so ungrateful" Eliamma retorted " We ate a lot of kappa of hers. She was a great help for us when we had no money. Don't forget that. God will curse ungrateful people."

Michael did not respond to his mother's angry words. He just kept quiet   and walked out of the room. That was his nature. He never argue with anyone. He would always openly express his opinion to anyone, whether they like it or not. If opposed, he would never respond. He would just walk out. That was his habit from early childhood.

Eliamma was wonder - struck about why Michael was angry with Sarada. When he was studying in Tenth standard and preparing for his final examination, Eliamma sent him to Sarada teacher for tuition, since he was weak in Malayalam Grammer. It was suggested by Sarada herself. Tuition was taken in Sarada's house at night. Only very few days Michael had attended the tuition. One day abruptly he came back home without attending the class.

"I don't want her tuition." He said angrily.

"Why? What happened? Her classes are wonderful I heard?" Eliamma asked

" I don't like her" He growled.

"But Why"? Eliamma asked.

 But Michael kept mum, and his mother knew there was no use in compelling him to disclose the reason. If he does not want to reveal he would never tell.

"Sister Eliamma, what to tell? Your son Michael is very sensitive. I had advised him very affectionaltly to study well. He is every brilliant. If he would put a little more effort I am sure he could get first class in the examination. But he did not like my advices. He got annoyed." That was Saradas explanation When asked by Eliamma about the withdrawal of Michael from her tuition.

Eliamma apologised for the ungrateful action of her son.

"Oh...that's allright. Your son is like my son. I have no grievances against him. In fact I like him, more than Martin."

Martin was entirely a different person. Though he was not good at studies, he was very active in extra curricular activities. He was very talkative and very pro -active in all other activities. If he is at home the entire area would vibrate with his voice. But Michael's presence would never be known. His voice would never be heard outside.

Eliamma purchased a Tiffin box for Martin to take his lunch to School.

"No Amma, I won't take rice to school. My friend Ouseph is bringing Kappa for his lunch. I don't like to eat rice sitting by his side while he takes kappa. I will go to hotel and take two dosa and one glass of butter milk, and that would be sufficient for me." Martin suggested.

Eliamma gave him thirty paisa for his lunch expense. Later that became a routine.

Martin never ate Dosa at hotel alone. He took three dosas wrapped in a paper and brought to his class room to share it with Ouseph. He took his share of kappa from him. Then that also became a routine till they finished their High School studies.

They had to walk three kilometres every day from home to school. Walking by the East river bank road was very pleasant; though it was a country road. The scenic beauty of river front was eye catching. The river waves change colour as the sunrays fall on them. Some time the river flows with glittering silver waves. Sometimes the water would look like blue velvet carpet spread wide. At dusk just before the Sunset, the waves would be red in colour. But during monsoon season the colour of the water would be muddy and the flow and current would be fierce.

The road divides at Mundalam Junction as " Kizakumbagam' (East bank) and Padinjarekara (west bank) There was Panchayat ferry, near Mundalam Junction.

In the evening, after the classes, Martin and Ouseph would walk together up to Mundalam Junction, where, Ouseph turns to right and part to fetch the ferry to cross the river to go to his house. Further ahead of a few meters, at the convent junction, Radha would be waiting for Martin . From there they walk together holding their hands together, and it was also a routine.

One day, evening, Eliamma and Sarada were standing in front of 'Manassery Poultry' looking at the chicks and talking on its further expansion and development. Both of them had seen Martin and Radha coming together from School. Both of them were in a very joyous mood and they were laughing aloud. They had noticed Martins left hand was on the shoulder of Radha and Radha's right hand was around the waist of Martin. Eliamma's face fell. Both the mothers looked at each other. Their minds were whirling with multiple thoughts.

"Radha has grown very fast. She needs a shawl." Eliamma suggested thoughtfully.

Sarada never expressed any anxiety or uneasiness. She said smilingly."They match well, don't they Eliamma?"

Eliamma did not answer. She was worried.

CHAPTER FOUR

TURNING POINTS

The result of the Government controlled public examination, SSLC, for the year 1959 was published in all news papers. Pala High School scored seventy five percentage of 'Pass'. There was only one 'First Class' from Pala High School. That was for Ouseph, son of the grave digger Pathrose, from the pulaya community. Name of Ouseph was highlighted with special comments in separate column in news papers. They wrote. "Promise of the future.''.

Martin's number was missing from the "Pass List". That was not expected by any one, except Martin. Though he had done well in all subjects, Science was written poorly. He was weak in science.

On knowing the result, Michael rushed to Mundalam to take Martin along with him to Cochin.

`"There is a very good tutorial college at Fort Cochin, very near to the house where I am living. Martin can stay with me and attend the classes."

Michael's suggestion was acceptable to Eliamma, his mother.

"But Amma would be alone here." Marin objected.

"Oh… That is not an issue. I will be fully engaged with my chicks and poultry works, Moreover, Sarada has arranged a servant girl for me to assist in poultry. She would come tomorrow and stay with me, so there would not be any problem. You go with your brother and study well, my dear son." Eliamma consoled him.

Prior to leaving Mundalam, Martin went to Ouseph's house to bid farewell.

"It is good that you are going to study at Cochin. Study well and get through the exam. As you are there please try to get a job for me. Any job would be fine for me. I heard that there are   lot of headload workers at Cochin. Some how I also want to get out of this place. I am fed up here." Ouseph requested. He seemed to be upset and worried.

" I will try through Michael. Surely some thing well hook up." Martin promised. When they hugged each other, Martin felt two drops of tears falling on his shoulders from Ouseph's eyes. That hurt him.

Ouseph had to survive. He did not wait for Martin's call. He was moving around Rubber Plantations, and Tapioca groves in search of labour jobs. Digging of mud with spade, and carrying heavy loads were the works he could get. Two rupees was the prevailing daily wage. Out of his remuneration, he used to give one rupee daily to his father Pathrose. Balance one rupee was just enough for him to survive for one day without starving. He started eating rice gruel and Kappa curry from local hotel, which cost only twenty five paisa. Lunch or dinner with rice and side dishes would cost more and such meals were luxury for him.

■■■

Michael was staying as a 'paying guest' in " Mana", Advocate Sankara Narayanan's house at Fort Cochin, near 'Amman Coil Temple'. Mana was a two storied building with two rooms up stairs. The staircase to first floor was constructed outside the house. Advocate Sankara Narayanan was collecting three rupees per month from Michael as rent. Though it was said to be 'Paying Guest .' no food was provided. Not even a cup of tea. He allowed Martin also to stay with Michael with an additional rent of two rupees and it was affordable for Michael.

The house owner Advocate Sankara Narayanan was living with his family downstairs. There were many rooms in the'Mana'. His wife Bhagerathy Amma was a noble lady. Michael and Martin were addressing her 'Ammai', means Aunty and she liked it. She had two pretty daughters of forteen and twelve years of age, Sobha and Prabha. They were students of Convent School studying in eighth and sixth classes.

When Advocate Sankara Narayanan happened to see the mark list of Martin he was astonished. Martin had scored above eighty percentage of marks in all subjects, with hundred percentagein mathamatics. But for science only twenty five percentage, the cause of his failure.

"My God, if you had scored at least pass marks in science you would have achieved ' First Class." I think you need not waste your time as a day scholar in Tutorial College. You need to attend only evening class for the failed subject. Day time you can go for a job, and make some money." Advocate suggested.

"Sir can I get a job with this failed certificate.?" Martin asked anxiously.

"Why not.? Almost all shipping companies are running short of staff to work in the wharf. I will take you to Brunton Company tomorrow. The works manager D'souza is a friend of mine." He said.

That was a big turning point in Martin's life.

It was like a dream for Martin and Michael when Martin got the job as a Tally clerk in "Brunton Company". His job was to take stock of materials unloaded from ships. The salary fixed for him was three hundred rupees per month for eight hours job a day. In addition, he would get overtime wages of three rupees per hour. Martin was doing three to four hours overtime everyday ignoring his evening classes. He was working very hard and was well appreciated by the management. They made him a permanent staff with increased salary and allowances.

****

Ouseph got depressed. He lost all hopes in life. He works the whole day, however, he didn't get enough for a decent life. That was the situation. He was ready to do any work. yet, many days he didn't get any work. He used to wander around the plantations for job , with a spade on his shoulder.

One day he did not get any work. He felt desperate. He went to river bank and sat on a rock at the ghats. The glittering waves of unending flow of the river consoled him. But his stomach was burning with hunger. He started to weep. Gradually the weep turned to a cry. The sound of his cry was echoed on the river spread.

"Ouseph…"

He heard some one shouting his name from the distance. Who could be that? He turned back and saw the Sexton Pappachan was approaching him. Sexton used to call him only when someone died in the parish. Ouseph had to search and find out his father Pathrose and make him to dig the grave in the Cemetery. It was not that easy to locate Pathrose. He would be lying some where fully intoxicated and   in a semi conscious condition. He had to drag him to Cemetery and make him dig the grave. Most of the time Ouseph himself had to dig. Three rupees was the meed for digging a grave. Some people wouldgive more. Some would try to skip after the funeral without paying the meed to the grave digger.

"What is the matter Mr. Pappachan " Did someone die?" Ouseph asked, thinking to dig the grave himself.

"Hay, it is not that. Nobody died. There is a letter for you from your friend Martin from Cochin. The postman gave it to me to hand it over to you."

He handed over a thick envelop to Ouseph and left. That was the first time in his life, Ouseph was getting a postal letter in his name. He read his address legibly written in Martin's handwriting which was very familiar to him.

"P.P.Ouseph, Palliparambil House Son of Pathrose, Behind Catholic Church, Mundalam P.O., Pala" The envelope was heavy. He opened the letter. It was a six page letter neatly written by Martin.

"From : Matrin Manassery,   Assit.Shipping Executive, Brunton company Ltd, Willingdon Island, Cochin – 3

 Date ; 01.06.1959

My dear friend Ouseph.

I am sorry, it took months to write you a letter. I wanted to write to you with some good news. Hence the delay. Today the good news has come. You are appointed as a Shipping clerk in my Company with immediate effect. I had submitted an application on your behalf for the job two months ago. My manager is a Brahmin and he did not like a Scheduled Caste person working in his department. He is conservative in his thinking. Then I approached my General Manager. He is an Anglo Indian.   Though he is an   arrogant   fellow, he was very considerate. When he came to know that you had passed SSLC with First class, he issued the appointment order immediately. Anyway it is through now and you can come and join immediately. On receipt of this letter you must start immediately from there. Your starting salary would be Three hundred rupees per month.'' Ouseph was thrilled. He got up from the rock, where he was sitting, and raised both of his hands up, and looked up to the sky with tearful eyes. He shouted loudly. "Thank you Jesus. Thank you"

He stood silently for sometime and murmured to himself. "At last God heard my prayers. Seen my tears. He released me from starvation, shame and dishonor". After wiping out the tears from his eyes he started to read the rest of the letter.

"My brother Michal and I are staying on the first floor of an advocate's house called Mana, at Fort Cochin on a monthly rent of five rupees. There are two rooms and a bathroom. We use one room as kitchen, and the other as our bed room. We sleep on the floor on grass mats. Today I bought one more mat for you for fifty paisa. you can share the bed room with us.

Cochin is a very different place than our Pala. The lifestyle of the people itself is different. Initially I felt a bit difficult to adjust with the city life. Now I am accustomed with it.

Though Cochin city is situated by the seashore,the atmosphere comparatively is very warm than our place. The air at Pala is very refreshing and the breeze is cool and smoothening. But here it is different. The air has a foul smell. Water that we drink at home is clear and pure. Here we have to drink pipe water with chlorine smell. There we are accustomed in open air bath in pure cool divine water of Meenachil river. Here we have to take bath in closed insular bath room. You may please start immediately on receipt of this letter. I know you have not travelled out of Pala in your life. I will write to you in detail on how to reach here.

Don't get panic. There is a bus from Pala to Kottayam at 6.30 in the morning. Get on the bus and get down at Etumannur. The bus fare is fifty paisa. You have to walk two kilometer distance from Ettumannur town to Railway station. That is not a big issue for people from Pala. We are accustomed to walking miles. But here at Cochin walking is a big issue. There are plenty of Cycle Rikshas here. For one kilometer ride we have to pay twenty five paisa.

There is a train at 9^0 clock to Ernakulam, coming from Kottayam. There is only five minutes stop at Ettumannur station. The train fair is Ninety paisa. Remember, you have to take ticket from the counter before boarding the train. By 12 º clock the train will reach at Ernakulam. Again there is a two kilometer walk from railway station to boat jetty. There are frequent boat services from Ernakulam to Cochin. Boat charge is twenty five paisa. There is a forty five minute boating to reach Cochin through the back waters. The boating will be a new experience for you. I am sure you will enjoy it. Boat would go very close to big ships; anchored at the wharf and moored in the lagoon.

There would be hundreds of sea gulls, floating on the back waters. They won't fly away even when the boat approaches them. Passing through the flocksof beautiful birds would be another unforgettable experience. Just opposite to Mattanchery Boat Jetty, there is a hotel named "Lucky star" You may have your lunch from the hotel. One meal with, fish curry, would cost you fifty paisa. Again two kilometer walk to Fort Cochin. Just walk straight through Palace road, which is one of the busiest roads in Cochin, and you will reach Amman coil Temple. Just opposite that temple you will find, a green painted house with a name board in written the front "Adv.Sankara Narayanan. B.A, LLB". That is the house. The house name "Mana" is also written on the gate pillar.As you enter the gate, you will find a concrete staircase to the first floor. We live there.

You must have at least forty rupees with you for the travel and for one months food expenditure. I will spare some money for you when you come here. You will get salary only after one month. Fifth of every month is the salary day.

One thing I will tell you Ouseph. Our Pala is a heaven when compared to this big city. Anyway, whereever we are, we have to live. Please start immediately. I will wait for ou.

With warm regards,

Your friend,

Martin Manassery

Until he reached the last part of the letter, Ouseph was thrilled. But the last part made him upset. His face fell. He started shivering.

Making forty rupees!? How could he make such a big amount!

He looked at the sky and let out a deep   sigh. Tears came down from

his eyes.

****

CHAPTER 5

HUMILIATION AND INSULT

Martin's letter made Ouseph helpless. He became desperate and upset. He was not sure what to do. Some how he had to make forty rupees. At least thirty would do. But how?

What was eft in his pocket was thirty five paisa! He thought of buying some snacks from hotel with that coins, so that he could manage his lunch and dinner.He was fed up of eating Kappa. A sort of despair developed in him to eat Kappa after he started taking food from hotel. He thought of Sarada teacher. She was a rich lady in the neighbourhood. If asked surely she would oblige with money. But in return he would have to pledge his self respect and integrity which he was not prepared to. He hated to go to her again. A hatred had developed in him after his short acquaintance with her.

One month back he had worked for five days in her plantation. She was converting her tapioca grove into rubber plantation. For that, a lot of spade works   had to be done. Five other people also were working in the enclosure.

But Ouseph was assigned in her vegetable garden for manuring. She also came to help him, which was very unusual.

It is a wonder, that you got first class in SSLC Examination." Sarada told him while she was helping him for manuring.

"What's the use teacher, My destiny is for manual labour" Ouseph lamented.

"Hay, manual labour is not that bad. One way it is better than white collar jobs. You will get three to four rupees a day. That makes nearly a hundred rupees a month. If you work in a shop for writing or billing, you won't get that much. Hardly you may get sixty or seventy. Sarada consoled him.

"My friend Martin is getting three hundred rupees."

"Oh…his case is different. He was lucky to get a job in ship."

"I had requested him to arrange me a job at Cochin."

"Hay Ouseph, You don't go. I will give you five rupees a day. you can have food also from here. You can consider this house as your home. "

That surprised Ouseph. What a great lady! All his ill thoughts about her were wrong . It might be out of misunderstanding by believing all kind of gossips about her!

Then it happened unexpectedly!

Sarada touched his armpit and said. " You are too young. Still you have a lot of hair here. Why don't you shave it off. I will give you a good shaving set. It is foreign made. Do you want a try?"

Ouseph felt ashamed and felt very discomfort to look at her face. He never expected her to talk in such an indecent manner.

That day Sarada teacher served him Rice and fish curry for lunch in her kitchen. Other workers were given food in the enclosure under the shade of a mango tree.

Radha was not   at home. Sarada sat by the   side of him and fondled his arm muscels and said."What a strong muscels you have! How could you develop such strong muscels at this young age? It is a wonder."

Ouseph felt a horripilation all over his body.

"Teacher, I am socked in sweat." He objected.

"I like the sweat of man." She put her arm around his neck and kissed his arm.

"When I am in sweat I don't like anyone touching me. " He said with irritation.

He finished his food quickly and got up. He was running away from the kitchen, like a frightened kitten.

That day evening before closing the work, Ouseph   was called to Kitchen. Sarada's voice was frantic in nature. Ouseph hurriedly went to kitchen running.

Sarada was standing, by drying her lengthy curly hair after a bath. She was wearing a wet thin linen long cloth around her waist and rest of the body was merely bare. She was trying to hook her brasiers behind, by stretching her arms behind. By seeing the peculiar situation Ouseph turned back to withdraw.

"Hay Ouseph, don't go. Please help me to hook this brasiers. It is a new one. That's why it is very tight . I can't fetch the hook. Please hook it for me." She pleaded.

Ouseph became perplexed. Though, he went behind her. With a reluctance he touched the belt of the brasiers. Suddenly she turned towards him, caught hold of him, and embraced him tightly. The brasiers fell on the floor and her bare heavey breasts pressed against his body hard. Her grip was very strong. Ouseph was stunned !

"Ouseph hold me…..hold me   tight. I want you.. I like you" she murmured with heavy panting.

Ouseph had to exert force to wriggle out from her wild witchy grip. He ran out of the kitchen with hatred and fright, and left the place.

Next day he received a five Rupee note sent by Sarada as his meed through another worker.

"You are wanted urgently by Mam" the worker said.

"I have some other job to do." Ouseph told him.

He never went to Sarada's garden for any work again. He never revealed the incident to anyone either.

Ouseph was pretty sure that he could get forty rupees from Sarada teacher if he went to her and ask. But he thought against it. He had never betrayed his conscience ever before. Not intend to betray in future too.

He requested sexton Pappachan to help him by a loan of forty rupees. He had shown him the letter from Martin.

"It is very good that you are getting a job at Cochin. But I am really helpless. What I can give you is a maximum of five or six rupees. Don't you know what I am getting from the Church. Only thirty rupees a month. I have requested the Vicar to increase my salary at least to hundred rupees. I also have to feed my family. The Vicar knows that I have no other income other than my salary of thirty rupees. He is like an offering box. Only inputs and no out put. Any way, you may try your luck with our Vicar Fr. Zacharias. If he is in good mood he may help. Please try." Sexton Pappachan advised.

Ouseph was afraid to approach Fr.Zacharias, the Vicar as he knew, the Vicar very well. He was a born conservative, and a hater of low caste community in general. He won't allow any black skin man go near him. Always he looked at them with dislike.

Three years back, Fr.Zacharias, the Vicar had announced in the Church during his sermon, that boys studying in High School and who wanted to become 'Altar Boys' to give their names to sexton. Accordingly seven boys, including Martin and Ouseph gave their names to Sexton. Next Sunday prior to Mass the Vicar asked the boys who gave their names to become Altar Boys, to be lined up in front of the Altar. The Vicar noticed Ouseph was standing among the seven volunteers. His face become reddened with anger. He pointed his finger at Ouspeh and shouted.

"You, Ouseph, who told you to be in this group?. You cannot become an Altar Boy. If you become an Altar Boy, who will assist Pathrose to dig the grave? Me? You may go back. You are not eligible. Your name is rejected. I need your services only in cemetry."

When all in the church laughed aloud, Ouseph came out from the group and ran out of Church crying.

Therafter, he never entered the Church, whenever people were inside.

However when no one was inside, he used to enter the Church, kneel in front of the idol of St. Mary, and weep by folding his hands. He had only three things to pray. Save him from humiliation and insult. Grant him an opportunity to live with self respect.

"Save me mother….Save me." He wept.

Some how he had to make forty rupees to go to Cochin.

He went to the presbytery, adjacent to church and knocked at the door of Father Zahcharia's room, very reluctantly and frightfully.

"Who is it?" Arrogant voice of the Vicar was heard.

Ouseph pushed the door open a little and showed his face.

The priest was sitting on his chair behind his desk and was counting moneys. It might have been that day's collection from offerings.

He saw Ouseph.

"You wait there, wait there. Don't come inside.I will come to you." The priest said with an irritant tone.

He got up from his seat and went to the door and asked. "What do you want Ouseph?"

"Father, I have got a good job at Cochin. Our Martin Manassery had arranged it for me. He wrote me to go to Cochin quickly. I have no money to go. I want forty rupees, Father. I will return it immediately when I get my first salary."

Ouseph said in one go. He took out the letter, from his pocket and extended to Vicar.

Father Zacharias looked at the youth with disgust. He did not take the letter

"Dou you think I am printing notes here." He asked arrogantly ?

"If you go away, who   will help your aged drunken father Pathrose? Who will help him in Cemetery? I order not to go. You   continue to work in cemetery. I will fix thirty rupees per month as your monthly salary as a special case. Over and above you will get three rupees per funeral as allowance. If you are lucky there would be more funerals.

You can have your dinner daily from my kitchen. As you know, my food is coming from convent. Most of the days there is a lot of food going to waste basket to be thrown out for stray dogs. Wasting of food is sin. It is God's gift. Today onwards you can collect all the left out food after my dinner and take it home.   Let Pathrose also eat some good food." What else do you require?"

Ouseph was hurt very deeply

His heart was pierced with sharp arrows of humiliation and insult.

His eyes filled, lips trembled.

"Thank you father."   he said politely, and walked away.

■■■

CHAPTER 6

GLITTERING BANGLE

Next day morning a nose piercing horrible smell spread in the west bank of Meenachil river in Mundalam village . The source of smell was from an abandoned well situated in the rubber plantation of 'Chackala Tomy.' Tomy was one of the richest men of Pala region. He was the trustee of Mundalam Catholic Church and a best friend of Fr.Zacharias .

It was suspected that the foul smell emitted from a decomposed corpse of some wild boar or a stray livestock, fallen in the deep well. The grave digger Pathrose , butcher Kather and Post Mortem Bhaskaran were called and entrusted with the job of taking out the decomposed corpse, and bury it. They demanded a meed of rupees fifty each and three bottles of country liquor in advance. It was given immediately without any bargain. The neighbours, watched from distance, the three drunken men descending in to the well   by rope. Within a few minutes one of them, grave digger Pathrose, came out of the well hurriedly and shouted aloud.

" That is not boar or cattle. It is Rosykutty, Tomy's wife…."

The entire village was shocked by the news. News spread like wild fire and all gathered at site. They peeped into the well by covering their nose and went back quickly. All had seen the decomposed body floating above the water about fifty feet below.

Many rumors spread. Some said that Rosykutty was murdered by her own husband. The second suspicion was that she had committed suicide.

Thresia, the maid servant of Tomy, had substantiated the second suspicion.

Rosykutty was sick and bed ridden for a few weeks. Last week she was taken to Kottayam General Hospital and diagnosed with abdominal cancer. It was a shock to everyone. Three days back she had expressed her desire to attend a retreat at Baranamganam Assisi Monastery. Tomy did not agree. The next day she was found missing. All thought that she might have gone for retreat alone. Nobody thought that she would end up her life in the deep well.

Thresia's story was convincing to all. " Poor Rosykutty. She could not bear the shocking news of her illness." They commented.

The body was taken out of the well wrapped in a bed sheet. Atmosphere of the entire village was filled with the stinking smell. The body was fully decomposed and swollen. The skin was peeling out from the body. There were wriggling of worms in the eyes, nose and ears.

All were in a hurry to bury the body immediately. A coffin was brought and the swollen body was squeezed in it with great difficulty and some how they could close the lid.

Pathrose was fully intoxicated and he could not stand on his legs. Ouseph was compelled to dig the grave in the cemetry, alone. He was disgusted and he cursed his fate.

Fr. Zacharias did not go to Chackala Tommy's house to recite the funeral prayers. He told Tomy to take the coffin straight to cemetery. Very few accompanied the coffin. Whoever accompanied, walked a few meters away from the coffin due to the unbearable foul smell.

Ouseph was standing by the side of the newly dug grave and his father Pathrose who squatted down on the floor was tired and boozy.

The coffin was placed by the edge of the grave and the pallbearer moved away quickly.

Fr. Zacharias, came along with sexton Pappachan to Cemetery wearing his ceremonial or religious garments. Sexton was carrying a Prayer book and the holy water sprinkler in his hand. Both of them fitted face masks to protect themselves from the foul smell. After reciting prayers quickly, the priest asked Ouseph to remove the lid of the coffin to sprinkle the holy water on the dead body. When the lid was removed, the people who stood at a distance moved further back ward. The priest and sexton turned their heads away while holy water was sprinkled on the dead body.

"Close the lid… Close the lid" The Vicar said loudly and walked away. The Sexton followed him.

Ouseph found it difficult to close the lid of coffin alone. People who were standing as spectators turned back and walked away .

"Come on Appa. For heaven sake please come and help me   to close this bloody lid Appa…" Ouseph shouted at his father in fury .

Pathrose sat deaf looking down. Ouseph had to close the lid himself. He found it difficult as a hand of the corpse was protruding out of the coffin. He had to hold the decomposed hand and pushed it hard to tuck it inside the coffin. The hand was oily and slippery. The peeled skin stuck in his palm. Somehow he could close the lid with great difficulty. There was no one to help him to descend the coffin in to the grave with rope..   With all his might he pushed the coffin into the grave. The heavy box dropped inside the grave. It hit the bottom one side down with a wild voice. The corpse fell out of coffin. He picked up the shovel , threw the mud very swiftly and closed the grave quickly.

It was six o' clock in the evening when Ouseph came out of the cemetery. He found the dusk was fast approaching. The entire area was deserted. There was no one in the enclosure, or in the court yard of the Church. He had seen his father Pathrose walking away with wavering steps. He was singing a funeral song loudly with intangible words.

" Alas : remember Men, remember all.

  Death will catch you unexpectedly

  All your bad deeds will accompany your soul.

And witness against you, in Holy court.

  All your wealth and   fame will never go with you.

Always do good things in your life."

Ouseph entered the Church. The interior was dark. Only A small lamp was glowing in front of the statue of St.Mary . He knelt down before the idol and wept for some time. His   mind was in pitch darkness. In that darkness a glimpse of gold bangle emerged out. He remembered where he had seen that gold bangle. It was on the wrist of the decomposed, swollen hand of the corpse he had buried a few minutes back.

That hand was protruding out of the coffin to make him difficult to close the lid of the coffin. When he caught hold of the slippery hand and forcibly pushed it into the coffin he felt the hardness of the bangle. He had seen the glimpse of the gold almost covered with the swollen fresh.

His mind worked very fast. A lightning passed through his brain. He started shivering. A determination projected in his mind. Why not to re- open the grave and remove the bangle   from   the hand of thedecomposed body. Perhaps, she might have worn on a waistchain on her loin. If he could take out the ornaments from the grave all his problem would be solved.

"Never steal someone's property even if you have to beg.

His father's advice echoed in his conscience.

 Oh. No!. That cannot be considered as theft. That gold is no man's property and it is far below in the grave. Even God has no right on that property. Grave digger is its custodian. He has all the right to take it.

He looked at the idol of Mother Mary again.

"Oh.. Mother! thank you for showing me the way to get out of this wretched cemetery life."

With a strong determination he went out of the Church.

CHAPTER 7

SIGH OF RELIEF

When Ouseph came out of cemetry it was dark. A few lights in the court yard and in presbytery were glowing. When he was about to go out of the gate, a roaring Jeep passed by and halted in front of the presbytery. A middle aged European jumped out of the jeep and stood looking around. He was wearing black pants and a white slacks. Ouseph noticed a clergy collar around his neck, and understood the visitor was a priest.

Fr.Zacharias came out of his room running, to receive the guest. They shook hands and talked a while. The jeep driver dragged out a heavy leather box by from the jeep. He took his taxi fare from the European Priest and drove off scanning its head light beam on Ouseph.

Fr.Zacharia had   seen him and called him by shouting his name.

" Hay Ouseph."

Ouseph ran to him and stood in front of the priests respectfully. The Vicar did not ask him   why he was there at that time of the night. He was son of a grave digger and he has the right to be near the church and cemetery at any time.

" It is nice that you are here now. Please take this box and keep it in our guest room. You know which is the guest room, don't you.? It is at the far end of the Varanda, next to my bed room". Vicar said to him as if an order.

Ouseph tried to lift the box. It was very heavy.

"Somebody has to help me to lift it on   to   my head." Ouseph said loudly. His voice showed irritation.

"Why not. I will help you."The white skinned priest said in pure Malayalam.

Ouseph was shocked and   understood   that the priest was a   Keralite. He carried the box on his head and walked along the Varanda. He was murmuring curses to himself as he was deadly tired. He thought of having a heavy dinner from the hotel that night with the meed he received from the funeral.

The door of the guest room was closed, but not locked. He pushed the door open with a kick by his foot. He had seen the coat, in the dim light of the room and dropped the box on it.

"You idiot, you should not have dropped the box." Fr. Zacharias shouted.

"Someone could come and help me to unload the box from my head." He shouted back and walked out.

" That lad is, I bet, an arrogant type." The guest priest commented.

"That is the general attitude of these subaltern caste people. They are always rebellious. They can be controlled only by harsh treatment." The conservative priest said loudly with an intention of Ouseph to hear.

He heard of course, but walked quickly towards the gate without bidding a farewell to Vicar

"Call him back. I have to give him a tip." Fr. Luiz, the visitor said in a hurried voice.

"Let him go….Let him go. No need to   give him any tip. He   is a worker in our cemetery and defiant in nature…" Fr.Zacharias said.

Rev. Dr. Luiz, SDA, who visited Mundalam Church, was the Rector of SDA Seminary in Rome. He belonged to SDA Congregation – "Servants of Divine Altar."

There are numerous Congregations   for   priests and nuns in Catholic Church and each Congregation' has its own moto and charism. Most of them are service oriented, like missionary works, Educational, Medical, Evangelization etc. SDA, 'Servants of Divine Altar' was a separate group established in Rome under the patronage of Pope himself, to select youth from the weaker sections of the society from all over the world and train them to be ordained as priests. Priests from SDA congregation would be deputed wherever shortage of clergies were reported.

There was shortage of aspirants in almost all seminaries all over the world. It was because of, as Pope pointed out in his circular to churches, the ideological and devotional deficiency amongst the priests. Priests considered themselves to be a separate and superior group and they tried to become a separate society within the Church. They maintained a comfortable distance from the laymen. Deficiency of " living ideal priests" to show an example to the new generation was the real problem. Priests became self centered and conceited, which ruined the basic concept of priesthood.

It was to train, spiritually sound and devotionally strong clergies, that the SDA congregation was established. The Congregation had its own seminary in Rome. Every year the Rector of the SDA Seminary used to visit poor Countries to select youngmen, to make them Aspirants.

Fr.Luiz was assigned by Pope to go to India to recruit young men and was directed to report to the Bishop of Pala. The Bishop asked Fr. Luiz to start his mission from Mundalam Parish.

Though Fr.Luiz looked like a European by his appearance and complexion, he was an Indian, haileing from Trichur. His parentage was not known to anyone. He was an orphan brought up in Don Bosco Orphanage. After his Matriculation he was taken by SDA fathers to Rome. He was ordained priest and,became the rector of the seminary, by the time he passed his post graduation and obtained Ph.D degree in Theology. That was his first visit to Kerala after becoming the Rector of SDA Seminary. He was longing to visit Don Bosco Orphanage Trichur, where he was brought up from infancy stage to adolescence .The orphanage was his parental house.

Fr. Zacharias gave him a warm welcome. He felt honoured to host one of the secretaries to Pope, Dean of the Altar boys of St. Peter's Basilica, and the Rector of SDA Seminary in Rome, under the Patronage of Pope.

"What a lucky man you are Fr.Luize. You could meet our Holy Father very often." Fr. Zacharia said with great admiration. " I have not seen a Pope, all my life."

They were sitting in the Vicars's office room.

"Oh… I meet Pope almost every day. I used to share his dining table. All Almost all Congregation heads staying in Rome have that privilege." Fr. Luiz said.

" Do you assist him in the Mass? " Zacharias asked very eagerly.

" There are Decons to assist Mass. I used to offer Mass along with him in his private Altar."

"Whoo..! that is great! really great! I never had a chance to meet Holy Father. It is a long cherished desire from my childhood. One day I will go to Rome and meet Pope." He said very thoughtfully.

"Even if you go to Rome, you won't be able to meet Pope personally. It is very difficult to get an appointment. Sometimes even Bishops have to wait for days to get an appointment. But you can see him from a distance on all Wednesdays, when he gives public appearance audience. He will pass through the crowd in an open jeep."

Fr. Zacharias sat looking at Luiz in astonishment and reverence.

"Fr. Luiz, I am lucky to have you as my guest. You are a person who has very close acquaintance with our Holly Father."

Zacharias wanted to know the daily routine of Pope and Luiz explained to him.

Some body   knocked at the door.

"Who is it?" Zacharias asked in an irritant tone. That was his nature.

Sexton Pappachan pushed the door open and entered.

"Hay, have you not gone home yet.?Vicar asked.

"I was in   front of grocery shop. They asked me whether you are available." I said yes and I came along with   them." Sexton said.

"Who"?

"Police."

"Police.Where? "

"They are in the courtyard. They asked me to inform you of their arrival. Waiting for your permission to come in."

"Why Police in here.What for?"Fr.Zacharias asked with an uneasiness.

"Father, they say, you have committed very serious criminal offence by allowing burial of the body of Tomy Chakala's wife who had committed suicide, without informing the Police. Shall I ask them to come in?"Sexton asked.

"What is the problem? Why Police?" Fr.Luiz asked.

The Vicar explained to him what had happened on that day, in brief.

"Oh my God. What a blunder you have done. Don't you know that it is against law ? " Fr.Luiz asked.

"Everybody knew it was a suicide. That lady could not withstand the mental strain, when she came to know that she was a cancer patient"

"What a meaningless justification Father. Once an unnatural death is occurred, the Police is to be informed immediately. Without a police clearance certificate the body cannot be buried. This directive is there in our Canon Law also."

Fr.Zacharias got frightened. He never had faced such a situation all his life

"Please ask them to come in." Fr. Luiz told the sexton.

Though there were five police men in the Police Jeep, only Inspector came in. He was a well practicing Catholic and had deep reverence for priests.

"Good evening Fr. Zacharias, I am Sub Inspector John from Pala Police Station." The Inspector introduced himself.

They greeted each other. Inspector was very happy to get introduced with a highly placed priest Fr. Luiz,from Rome. They talked about Pope and Rome for some time, and then came to the subject.

"What you have done is a very serious offence. It is a non bailable offence." Inspector said to Fr.Zacharias.

"I was ignorant about its seriousness and consequences. Can you help me.?" Zacharias was on the verge of crying.

"Don't worry Father. Our Circle Inspector is also a Catholic. We had a discussion with Pala Bishop about an hour back. It is decided not to make a FIR, and close the file after taking a written statement from you." Inspector said.

Zacharias let out a sigh of relief.

CHAPTER 8

ENCOUNTERING A DEVIL

Food for the Vicar of Mundalam Church was supplied daily from the convent. The sisters of the convent had considered   the supply of food to Vicar was their duty and taken it as their divine obligation. In return, the Vicar used to offer evening Mass daily in their Chapel. He was their confessor also. That was the practice being continued from the very inception of the convent which was very close to the church.

 The Mother Superior of the Convent heard the news from Pappachan the sexton, who was their caretaker of the cattle farm also, that the Vicar had a priest guest from Rome. Immediately she   arranged a special dinner for the priests. By eight O' clock the food was brought by the Sexton, and served on the dining table, at the Rectory.

Fr. Luiz was shocked when he saw so many different meat dishes served on the table. There were, duck fry, pork vinthalu, chicken roast and fish molly along with other usual local dishes.

"Oh my God! I won't eat any of these things at night. I need only two slices of bread and one banana. To wash it down, one glass of Milk would be fine for me" Fr. Luiz said.

Fr. Zacharias, the Vicar, was disappointed.

" Then who will eat all these food," He asked

"Better send it back to convent." Luiz suggested.

"Oh. No. They will get hurt. Let the sexton take it to his home,"
Fr. Luiz suggested .

Fr. Zacharias noded his approval with an unpleasant facial expression.

Fr. Luiz presented one bottle of Italian wine to Fr.Zacharias.

"This is the best wine and widely used in Italy. It is not like our Mass
wine. It possesses spirit and gives intoxication, if consumed more.
Small quantity is good for appetite, and health."

Zacharias wanted to have a drink on that day. He was deadly worried
and upset on the burial issue that occurred at noon. He was not aware of
its complications and after effects until the Inspector had told him.

" If someone would dig up the case on a later stage, and file a petition
to the court alleging that the death was a murder and that the corpse was
buried even without a postmortem, the Vicar also would be booked."
That was what the Police officer told before he left.

"Hope, that would never happen. " He further said, and that was a
caution!. That made Fr. Zacherias 'under his skin.'

Fr.Luiz was satisfied with two bananas and one glass of milk as supper. He did not even touch any of the dishes that were brought from the convent.

"I can't bear the chilly and hot spices. It would upset my stomach." He said.

Having consumed a glass of Italian wine, the appetite of Zacharias had flamed up. He ate more and drank more wine. He had forgotten, what Fr.Luiz had told him when he presented the wine bottle. "It possess spirit and gives intoxication if consumed more."

Fr. Zacharias consumed for rounds of wine. It hit him hard. He became fuddled and collapsed . With difficulty he could get up from his seat but could not make a step further even to wash his hand. He fell on the coat, without removing his slippers . He started snoring quickly.

Fr. Luiz got upset. With the help of sexton Pappachan, he cleaned the face and hand of the Vicar with a wet towel. " He never drinks. Takes a little wine when he eats meat." The sexton said. "Oh… I never knew." Luiz said sadly. "I doubt very much whether, he will be able to get up at five in the morning. He has to offer the Mass at Five thirty in the morning . I suggest you   may please   offer the morning Mass." Sexton suggested.

" That won't be a problem…You may please clear the table and switch off the light.   Please take all the   food to your home." Luiz instructed and left the room.

 He went to the guest room, sat on his bed and   started to recite the Rosary, his routine night prayer.

"Good night father"

He heard the shouting of sexton which interrupted his Rosary.   He watched the sexton leaving the premises through the window. He was carrying the food bags.

He looked at his watch. It was ten at night. Indian time is three and half hours ahead of European time. The time difference disturbed him to get to sleep. He used to go to bed when in Rome at ten thirty. It would be one thirty after mid night in India. Till that time he had to sit idle awaiting to get sleep. He had to get up at five in the morning for the five thirty Mass, as suggested by sexton.

All his routines were jeopardized. He felt disturbed.

In order to get a quick sleep, he started to read a book. But, could not concentrate in it due to the heavy sound of snoring of Father Zacharias from the adjacent room. That made him irritant. The snoring nocie was like the roarof a swine.

He got up restlessly from the bed, went out of the room   and started walking alongh the veranda, to and fro.

He felt lonely as the entire area was deserted. There was a crescent moon glittering in the sky playing 'hide and seek' game with the clusters of clouds. The moon was throwing its pale yellow   light everywhere. The church was situated in   the middle of a   rubber plantation. But, Fr. Luiz felt the church was in the middle of a thick forest. There was not a glimpse of   light anywhere in the vicinity. Not even a house   was seen even at   a far distance. A few fire flys were found flying aimlessly through the woods. There was a slight drizzling an hour before, that sprinkled rain drops all over the rubber trees. The wet green leaves glittered in the moon light like silver festoons and the sight was beautiful. Luiz enjoyed the scenic beauty of the terrane at night.

He heard a howling voice of a jackal somewhere in the distance. Suddenly a group of jackals from somewhere nearby started screaming together, created a horrid atmosphere. An owl flew very low, through the court yard and sat on a tree. It's loud humming was frightening.

Father Luiz was about to go back to his room. Suddenly he had noticed a movement   at the far distance of the rubber plantation, as if some one was walking. When looked curiously, he found someone or something was moving   towards the Church. Fr.Luiz was horrified when he saw a figure standingin front of the cemetery. He slowly pushed open the cemetery gate. Fr.Luiz   clearly heard the cracking sound, when the sorted steel gate was pushed open.

Luiz was frightened and he started sweating. He never believed in the movements of demon or evil spirit at night. When such stories were heard, he   used to reject them categorically and considered it as superstitions.   Now   an actual devil was right in front of him. He had to believe !

He wanted a help to face the devil. But from where ? Fr. Zacharias was off with booze. Sexton had already left. No other living soul was in the premises of the church. He entered his room, hurriedly opened his leather box, took out a .22 revolver and a small silver cross. Cross is the most powerful weapon to encounter a devil. Devils are afraid of Cross. They would flee away at the sight of a Cross .

 He prayed to the Holy Spirit for courage to encounter the devil. Then he   started walking towards the Cemetery, very cautiously.

Abruptly, the howling of wolves stopped. The owl also stopped its humming, as if they were all afraid of something.

With the cross in his left hand and .22 revolver in his right hand, he slowly approached the steel gate of the Cemetery.

CHAPTER 9

REFUGEE FROM CEMETERY

Fr. Luiz was shocked and horrified when he saw the 'devil' standing in the grave yard.

What he was expecting was a fierce looking ugly face, with fangs protruding out of the corner of its mouth. But what he saw was a young man, the same   irritant low caste black youth, who had carried his leather suit case to the guest room.

Fr. Zacharias introducing him as "son of the grave digger" and calling out "Ouseph."

Fr.Luiz wondered what the youth was doing inside the cemetery at that hour of night. Has he come to dig another grave for another burial ? But

Fr. Luiz did not hear of any death while he was with the Vicar and sexton for a   long time. If at all any funeral was scheduled for the next day, they would have discussed about it for sure.

 Fr.Luiz, put the cross in his pocket, and tucked the revolver under the shirt between his hip and pants belt. He hide himself behind the gate pillar and observed the movements of the youth, Ouseph.

Ouseph removed his shirt and hungd it on a wooden cross erected on a grave. He removed his long cloth also and put it over the shirt on the cross. He stood naked, wearing only his underwear. His black body was fully wet with sweat which was clearly seen in the moon light.

The youth stood watching a new grave before him on which there were a few wreaths with unweathered flowers.

Ouseph removed the wooden cross from the grave and placed it a few feet away on the ground very carefully. He also removed all wreaths one by one. He took a showel and started to dig open the grave quickly. Father Luiz could not believe his own eyes!. What the hell he is doing!. Why is he opening a grave at night? Luiz could not guess the motive behind. Within ten minutes Ouseph removed the heap of the mud from the grave.

 Luiz could not conceal his emotion and control the anxiety. He came out of his hideout behind the gate pillar, and walked slowly towards Ouseph.   Ouseph could not sense the movements behind him and continued digging.

"What are you doing." Luiz asked in a rough voice standing just behind him.

Ouseph was jerked by the shock and looked back frantically. He got frightened to death, when he saw the white skinned priest standing just behind him. The shovel fell from his hand. He knew he was caught redhanded.

He looked at the face of Fr. Luiz with widened eyes. They both stared each other for some time.

Slowly the expression of Ousepeh changed to hysterical. His eyes filled with tears. An utter desperation reflected in them. His cheecks became pale. His chin started to shiver.

He looked at the sky in despair and cried aloud as if he was accusing "Oh God, why did you deceive me?. Will you not allow me to escape from this cemetery life?. Am I destined to end up the life in this grave yard?. Yes. I will end up my life. I will commit suicide...I will commit suicide."

His voice was very hoarse and fierce. The sound echoed in the cemetery like thunder .

While crying aloud he beat his chest violently several times and pulled his hair hysterically. Luiz had to hold his hands to stop him from inflicting self injury on his body. His hands were strong like steel roads.

"Stop screaming like a beast." Fr. Luiz shouted at him.

Ouseph did not bother to obey him. He continued to cry aloud violently.

He knew he was caught and would end up in jail. He lost all his hopes. His screaming became uncontrollably wild.

Fr.Luiz gave slapped him on the face very strongly and raised his voice and shouted. "Stop it. Stop it, I say!"

His voice was very hoarse and it was a big psychological blow to Ouseph.

He stopped screaming abruptly and started shivering. He looked at Luiz with bewildered wide eyes.

 The   priest made him to sit on the ground. He also sat by the side of him, patting his back. Both of them were silent for some time.

Two bats were flying above them circling as if they were watching what was going on there in the cemetery.

"Sorry, I had to beat you." Luiz said in an apologizing manner.

"I deserve it." Ouseph said, sadly.

"Your name is Ouseph, am I right? I heard Fr. Zacharia's calling your name."

"Yes. I am Ouseph."

"Why are you reopening the grave.?"

Ouseph was silent.

"Tell me the truth. Why do you want to reopen the grave where a decomposed corpse was buried. Never heard of such a thing."

"I wanted to take the gold bangles from the hands of the corpse."

"Gold bangles.?"

"Yes. Gold."

"How do you know there is gold bangles, on the corpse?".

"I buried that corpse."

"Even if it is from a corpse or from the grave yard,it is steeling. It is a crime."

"Yes, I know."

"How many times have you committed such crimes.? I mean stealing."

"I never stole anything from anywhere in my life"

"What made you to do such a nasty stealing now.?"

"I got a job at Cochin. It is a golden opportunity for me to escape from this cemetery life. I wanted forty rupees to reach up to Cochin to take up   the   job. I asked everyone known to me. No body gave."

"You should have asked your Vicar. After all you and your father are serving for the church."

" I asked him. He said he was not printing currency."

That shocked Luiz. He felt annoyed on Zacharias and pitty on Ouseph.

"What job have you got at Cochin. Scavenger? Or Sweeper...? Watchman?

"No..Tally clerk in Bronton Company?"

"Tally Clerk?! That is a job connected with shipping.? That needs education and qualifications. Have you studied?"

Fr. Luiz expected a negative answer. In those days, low caste children were never sent to school.

When Ouseph said that he had passed SSLC with First class, the priest was astonished. He looked at the youth with a lot of admiration.

"You mean you have got first class in SSLC?"

"Yes Father, This year I am the only one in my school who got First Class."

" Does your Vicar know this?"

"Why not? All the world knew. My name was in all newspapers."

A low caste lad, that too the son of a grave digger,achieving, First class in SSLC? That was beyond imagination in those days.

"How did you get the job at Cochin?" The priest asked. "Nowadays it is very difficult to get a job in a Europien Company . Bronton Company is a world renowned firm."

"But what is the use? I am not in a position to reach Cochin and take up the job. I lost all my hope. It was my last attempt to make some money by taking out the gold from the decomposed corpse buried in the grave. If there had been any other source to get forty rupees I would have not attempted such a nasty job. You blocked that also . I will end up my life. Up on God, I will die myself. Surely I will hang my self ". Ouseph started to weep again.

"Hay..be courageous. For want of fourty rupees don't end up your life. I will give you forty rupees." Luiz said.

Ouseph looked at him anxiously.

"Don't worry, I will give you the money. Now, you may please redo the grave properly. Tomorrow if someone sees it, he should not have any suspicion." Fr.Luize advised.

Ouseph got up from the ground, picked up the shovel and started to re-heap the mud which was removed by him. Fr. Luiz sat there watching. When the earth was fully redone, Fr. Luiz got up and helped Ouseph to re position the cross and the wreaths in its original places on the grave

"OK. Now you dress yourself." Fr.Luiz asked him.

Then only Ouseph realized that he was naked and was wearing only his underwear. Suddenly he picked up his cloths, and wore them properly.

When they were walking out of the cemetery together, Luiz asked him." Tell me how you got the placement in Bronton Company?"

"Martin arranged for me."

"Martin? …Who is he."?

"He is my friend and classmate. He works there ."

He took out, Martin's letter, from his underwear pocket, and handed it over   to

Fr. Luiz.

"What is this.?"

" This is the letter from Martin. It is my placement order too.."

"Let us go to that light so that I can read it"

Fr.Luiz walked towards the court yard, where a bright light was glowing in front of the church. He sat on the cement steps of the church and asked Ouseph to sit near him.

He unfolded the letter and started to read.

They heard the clock inside the church ring twelve times. A nocturnal bird cried loudly and flews away from the roof of the church followed by another one. Ouseph kept on looking at them until they vanished in darkness.

CHAPTER 10

TURNING POINT

It was a great relief for Ouseph when Fr. Luiz promised him to give forty rupees to go to cochin, to take up the proposed job arranged by Martin. His frantic search for money had come to a happy end

To confirm what Ouseph said was true, Fr. Luiz went through Martin's letter, thoroughly.

Ouseph became impatient when Fr. Luiz took more time to read the letter. He thought the priest was delaying purposefully. A doubt crept up into his mind. "Can I believe this priest?" All priests are very good in delivering sermons, on the podium of the church and very poor in putting them in to practice.

He had seen dark clouds mounting up in the sky. The crescent moon had already vanished. The terrain was blanketed with darkness. A heavy rain could be anticipated. He wanted to reach his hut before the rain started. He was craving for a sleep. It was a tiresome day for him and never felt such an exhaustion ever before.

After reading the whole letter word by word Fr. Luiz looked at Ouspeh who was sitting on the cemented steps in deep thought and staring at the dark sky

"It is a nice letter. Well written. This Martin knows how to write." Fr.Luiz commented.

Ouseph did'nt look at him, but continued to stare at the sky.

"You should have shown this letter to Fr. Zacharias, your Vicar." The priest said.

Ouseph turned his head and looked at Fr. Luiz. "I have shown to him . He did not bother even to look at it." Ouseph said. There was a bitterness in his voice.

"Father, If you can give me that promised money, I will go. I think a heavy rain can be expected any time from now. You can also have your sleep." He said with irritation and urgency in his hurried voice.

Fr. Luiz looked at him and smiled "Hay Ouseph, you don't believe in Divine Providence?"He asked.

 Ouseph thought for a while and said." I don't know father. Somehow I am just pulling on with my wretched life. Struggling for my daily food, being ignored and deprived by everyone. A man like me can not even believe in the existence of God, leave aside the Providence. " The dejection in him was very clear in his words.

Fr.Luiz got shocked by his sharp reaction. He knew that emerged from his desperation.

" I know Ouseph you are living in utter poverty and hardship. Still you could complete your school studies. You could achieve First Class in SSLC Examination, that also with highest marks. That itself shows how much God loves you. Only because of the Divine Providence that you could achieve it. Without the providence…."

Ouseph did not allow the priest to complete. He interrupted with harsh words. "Will you stop this sermon please. I have heard a lot of such talks before. It never gave me any good. Such talks never quench my hunger. To put something into my stomach, I have to struggle hard. Still I was hungry always. If at all there is a God, a real God, in heaven, he won't have time to look at a penurious man like me. ''

His voice was harsh. The words were stubborn. His body language was rebellious.

Fr. Luiz realized the frustation and turmoil in his mind .

Ouseph was panting as if he had ran miles. After a few deep breaths and a sigh, his mind became calm, then, he realized that he would never have expressed his indignation in such a harsh manner to the priest. It might have made a hurt feeling in him. He may sometimes pull the rug out from under his feet. He may   withdraw his promise. In that case his last hope of getting money to go to Cochin would be lost for ever.

With a confusion and fright he looked at Fr. Luiz and pleaded."Sorry father. Out of my frustration I had blabbered something. Please forgive me. Please don't withdraw your offer. I have no other go. You are my last refuge." He was at the verge of a sob.

"The last and first refuge is God. Only God Ouseph."

Fr.Luiz moved closer to him and placed a hand over his shoulders. Ouseph felt a horripilation all over his body.

"Ouseph, shall I ask you something?" He asked.

"What is that Father?"

"You said just now, that God is sitting in heaven and has no time to look at your toil.

Tell me Ouseph, where the heaven is situated.?"

Ouseph remembered having read in the Bible that Christ will reappear along with an army of heaven through the clouds . But he knew that was all some sort of imagination. There can't be a heaven beyond the cloud and in ionosphere, or exosphere.

"It is in our mind". Ouseph said with a skepticism

"Absolutely correct. The heaven hell and purgatory etc… are all just in our mind."

Ouseph never expected such a statement from a priest.

"Now tell me where is your mind? " Fr. Luiz asked.

Ouseph said confidently. " It is here." He touched his chest .

Fr. Luiz smiled and said " No …….. That is your chest, and inside you have your heart. But your mind is situated inside your Glabella."

'Glabella?'' Ouseph got confused.

Fr. Luize, with his finger, touched the Glabella portion of Ouseph's head between the brows, below the fore head and said."Here is you nerve centre. Your mind and consciousness are situated here. Your heaven, hell and all your belief and superstitions are assimilated in here."

Ouseph touched his glabella and asked. "So. God also sits here . ''

"God is a power of nature. Your personal power is absorbed in your body. Like wise the power of nature is absorbed in the nature itself. The entire universe and all the substances were created and governed by this omnipotent and benevolent power. Jesus Christ called that power as 'Father' and taught us to call him 'Father'. The Heavenly Father. He won't sit anywhere. He exists everywhere like sun light. We live in the light. He governs everything and everyone with care."

"But why did he create people with discrimination.?"

"What do you mean?"

"Why did he discriminate people as rich and poor? When he gives wealth and food abundantly to rich, people like me are subjected to starvation. I think God has got no sense of righteoueness." There was a ridicule in his voice.

Fr. Luiz looked at him with great interest. The hatred towards his life and to the whole world was reflected on his face. His eyes were glittering with hatred.

"Son, God created everything   in this Universe with equilibrium and with exact balancing.   Just look at our earth, It is revolving in its correct rhythm in order to give us light,darkness,   day, night, climate change's etc. If the earth was not erected in a   particular slanting position, it would not have revolved at all. It is simple   physics. To erect the earth in its correct slanted position, it had to be statically balanced. For that, God has created and positioned mountains, hills and crests in its correct size and volume as well as weights. When man started to distruct or eradicate such balancing system by cutting down the forests, and blasting off mountains, leveling of hills and   lakes, what happens, do you know?, The balancing of earth gets disturbed resulting in climate variation and natural calamities. You can't blame God for such calamities and disasters. That is all the reciprocative actions of man's wrong doings. Do you agree with me?" Fr. Luiz talked as if he was lecturing in a class room.

"Yes. Father…" Ouseph said like an attentive student

"Likewise, the theory of humanism. Life is also reciprocative to each other. One to support and supplement the other. There are different types and kinds of people with different types of abilities and capabilities. When they all join together, a society is formed. God planned food and wealth equally for everyone. That have to be shared equally by everyone. When a few start to keep wealth and food for themselves, the socio economic equilibrium would get imbalanced. Whenever imbalance takes place, starvation and poverty will be the result. The imbalancing is created by man and not by God. God is not responsible for the discrimination amongst the people. For him all are equal."

"God can correct it." Ouseph argued.

"From time to time God gives wisdom to man,through wise men to correct themselves. Christ was born to correct the people. He taught righteousness to the world. He called for equality and Christians are called to practice sharing, equality and righteousness. But, now, even churches are engaged in mobilizing funds and amassing wealth." That is against Christian doctrine. Both the heaven and hell are within ourselves. They are the   stages of minds. Contentment is heaven. Discontentment is hell. Nothing else."

Ouseph was very attentive to the talk. His conversation was not like most of the other priests. They always try to hide the truth about God and Heaven and project an illusion or fantacy with appropriate Bible quotes!

"Father, as you said, if the heaven and hell are the frames of mind, a mental phenomina why at all the priests create a whimsy imagination in their preaching as if they exist. It is deceiving. Why at all we need the Altar, rituals etc? They are all mere superstitions, is int it?"

"They teach erroneously as they do not realize the truth. The Altar rituals etc are all needed to guide the people to the reality and truth. They are under the bondage of ignorance. It will take time for them to grasp the wisdom. One day the truth will relieve them. That's what Christ had said. Till then the Altar, rituals rites etc are to be continued. Only through them they could be guided to wisdom."

" Three years ago I wanted to become an Altar boy to serve God on the Altar. I was mentally prepared and was very eager to become an Altar boy. But I was thrown out by Father Zacharias as I belonged to a low caste backward community and son of a gravedigger. I was cruelly humiliated in public." Ouseph was panting heavily due to emotion when he remembered that incident.

Fr. Luiz was moved by hearing his emotional words.

"Do you want to serve at Altar?" He asked

"No Father. Not any more. Now I am grown up and not suitable   to become an   Altar Boy."

"Not as an Altar Boy; as a Priest, like me to serve at the Altar to serve the people and serve God. To preach and teach the actual doctrine of Jesus Christ."Fr.Luiz asked looking into his eyes.

Ouseph was shocked and overhwhelmed; He stood agape in wonder and disbelief."Am I worthy enough for that? " He asked

"You are an apt person to become a priest to serve God."

Ouseph could not believe what he had heard. He was stunned and perplexed. He could not say a word.

"I think, I was guided to visit this place to pick you up. It is God's will that you to become a priest. He calls you to his Altar to spread his doctrine of righteousness to the world "

"Am I worthy ofr that?" Ouseph   doubted again.

"Why not? You are the worthiest person to become a priest. You are qualified and choosen by God. If you become a priest, I will see that you would be appointed as Vicar at this Parish at least for a short period. You will listen to the confessions of the people who had accused you. You will bless the people who had insulted and cursed you. You will give Eucharist on their tongues who had denied your rights. That should be your revenge. A revenge for God and for good.

Ouseph felt like crying. His heart was throbbing violently due to an upsurge of emotion.!

`You were in search of forty rupees to go to Cochin to take up the job of a shipping clerk.   But God was in search of you to make you his missionary to spread his doctrine of righteousness."

Ouseph caught hold of the hand of Fr.Luiz and held it tighty to his chest, and wept. Fr.Luiz embraced him affectiontely.

CHAPTER 11

IN VATICAN

UK based "Brunton company limited" was one of the leading shipping companies working in Cochin during 1960's. They were steamer agents . Almost all huge ships anchoring at Cochin Port were under their agency contract. Steamer agents were fully responsible for the security and management of the ships under their agency, when the vessels were in the port.

Martin started his career as a Shipping clerk in Brunton Company. He was promoted as Shipping Executive,   after his probationary period. He was the youngest officer in the company.

His duty was to meet the captain of the ship, on behalf of the company, immediately on arrival of the vessel at the wharf. He had to make arrangements for oil refilling of the ship, and arranging 'shipstores' (Kitchen stores") and supervision of loading unloading. At his young age, they were heavy jobs but he was handling well and he was very hardworking. Management had a lot of appreciation on his performance. Company provided him a new cycle for his own use. He changed his pattern of dressing from long cloth and loose shirt to pants, full sleeved white shirt and black tie. He was allowed to wear company's crested cap which gave him a look of authority. The labour gang working in wharf and their 'Moopan' (leader) Hamza were addressing him 'sir'. He became very popular at Port and Customs.

That day, when Martin came from wharf after a hectic work, he found a blue air mail placed on his office table. It was a foreign envelop with multi colour boarder printing. He wondered who would be the sender as he had none to send an airmail from abroad. With mounting eagerness he picked up the envelop and looked at the 'from address': It read "Brother Ouso, Aspirants house, SDA Seminary, Cardinal Strada, 10 A, Vatican City, Italy. "   Underneath it was written in capital letters. 'OUSEPH.P.P' .

Martin was shocked and stunned for a while. He could not believe that Ouseph had reached Vatican! What a miracle.!

He felt guilty for not having remembered him . When Ouseph had not shown up for taking up the job, he was annoyed and irritated as he had taken a lot of strain to get the approval from his superiors for Ouseph's placement in the Company. ' Leech won't sleep in bed,' he thought in annoyance. After all Ouseph belonged to labour class and might have interest only in labour works. He might be wandering through estates in search of labour work, Martin thought, and ignored him

Martin used to visit his house at Mundalam very frequently . He was getting monthly off regularly, unlike   Michael. Management   of Michael was very stingy in giving leave to their employees.

Whenever Martin   reached home,   Sarada techer and her daughter Radha used to call on him. Radhha had a lot to talk about several subjects, non stop. She talked about everybody in the village except about Ouseph. Martin never enquired about him either.

During one visit, Martin had presented an Italian rold gold necklace with glittering black beeds to Radha.

"It is a foreign necklace. Never fades its colour. I got it from a ship." Martin said while presenting the necklace.

"Oh. It is beautiful." Radha exclaimed

"You can wear it on your wedding day." Sarada said admiring the workman ship of the necklace.

Radha was thrilled to have the necklace. She kept it as a precious treasure.

In his busy life, Martin had forgotten his friend Ouseph. All of a sudden, after a period of eighteen months, when he appeared in front of him in the form of an air mail, Martin became upset and he felt guilty for having forgotten him completely.

Now Ouseph is in Vatican! The hierarchical headquarters of Catholic Church, where the throne of St.Peter was installed, and where an ordinary man like Martin would never be able to visit.!

With mixed feelings of astonishment and anxiety Martin opened the envelop. There were four sheets of paper blue in colour, with a water mark of St. Peter's Basilica on which Ouseph had written very neatly with pen. A postcard size colour Photo also was enclosed.

Martin had a glance on the photo andhe got astonished. His eyes became widened due to bewilderment.

Ouseph was standing with Pope John, the Twenty Third. The Pope was holding his hand with a pleasant smile! There were two more Europian youths by the side of him. All the three youth were wearing dark blue suits, black ties and white shirts. There were identical giltted crest embroided on the breast pocket of their suits. The black skin of Ouseph was very prominent amoung the white people. His black skin had a special effect. Black also would be beautiful sometimes, he thought.

Martin read the letter with lot of curiosity and anxiousness.

"Vatican – 11.09.1960"

My dearest friend Martin.Praise be to the Lord.

One and a half years back you sent me a letter asking me to take up a job at Cochin. Fortunately by the grace of God, that letter turned out to be my Visa to Vatican.

I reached Vatican and joined as an Aspirant in SDA Seminary, eighteen months back. Everything happened like an accident, quite unexpectedly. It was God's Providence indeed!

Vatican City, as you know is a holy place for Catholics where Pope lives. Vatican City is an independent State, within the city of Rome, the smallest country in the world with an area of 0.44 square miles equivalent to 108 acres only. The city is famous for architecture, sculptures and paintings. The world renowned works of the great artists like Michaelangelo and Raphel are still intact in Vatican. Thousands of tourists visit Vatican everyday.

Our SDA Seminary is situated in Vatican and Rome as well. The school portion is situated in Vatican city in the enclosure of St.Peter's Basilica, but the boarding house is about one kilometer away in Rome.

In your letter you wrote to me to keep forty rupees with me when I go to Cochin for my one month's expenditure and travel. I did   not have even forty paisa then, and I was in frantic run to make that money. In that run   I met Fr.Luiz, the Rector of SDA Seminary. It was a very peculiar situation about which I can't write now. It is a stinking story.

Within twelve months I could learn Italian language. Now I can read and write Italian very fluently. Last month, me and three of my co-aspirants were selected as Altar Boys of St. Peter's Basilica, to assist at the holy Mass of Pope John XXIII. It was a great honour for a low caste man like me   to become an Altar Boy at St.Peter's Basilica.

Yesterday we Altar boys had the honour of having lunch with our Holy Father Pope, in his dining room. I had the privilege to be seated by the side of Pope. He loves Indians and he loves our country, India.

Though I was denied to enter the Altar of our Mundalam Church,   now I am blessed to be on the high Altar of St.Peter's Basilica, to assist our Holy Father for his Mass. My novitiate and training will be for a few more years. I will be ordained a priest and will be known as Fr. Ouso SDA. Fr.Luiz promised me that he would get me a short time "Visiting Posting" to our Mundalam church after my ordination. I am looking forward to those days. I want to offer a Mass at the Altar of Mundalam church where I was denied entry by Fr. Zacharias. I want to bless our natives who had ignored and insulted me. I want to hear the confessions of the people who ill-treated me. I want to serve the Eucharist to the people who condemned me".

Martin felt disgusted when he read the intentions of Ouseph, He wanted to avenge the natives who had disclaimed and condemned him in the past.

If he had the mentality to forgive, how great it would have been! Only a clean hearted person could become a good priest. He should be without any malice, treachery and evil intentions. Psalm teaches to pray, "Create in me a pure heart, O' God, and renew a steadfast spirit within me."

Christ said to 'follow' him with a clean heart after leaving everything behind that included all the mental agony and anxieties. Ouseph was carrying all his hatred in his broken heart along with him. Let God alone clean up his heart.

Ouseph, concluded his letter: " Martin, my father died last year. He was in hospital for months with ulcer, that's what Fr. Luiz told me. I did not go for the funeral, though Fr. Luiz had arranged plane ticket for me. Now I have none in Kerala except you. Please do write to me sometimes, whenever you are free. I will visit our native land only after my Ordination. I want to go there as a priest. Please do pray for me.

With love and prayers,

your friend Ouseph

That was the first and the last letter Martin had received from Ouseph from Vatican

CHAPTER 12

A Surprise Wedding

Within three years Martin became a well known shipping executive in Cochin port. He was the youngest executive in Brunton Company and was looking after shipping clearing works of the company in wharf. There would be always four ships birthed in the wharf and six ships moored in back waters. Martin was smart enough to attend the shipping clearing works on all the ships simultaneously with four gangs of labour force assigned under him. Hamza Moopan, the leader of labour gangs was very supportive to him (Moopan means leader)

One day Martin happened to see two counter foils of movie tickets in Michael's shirt pocket, when he had put aside the shirt to give to laundry.

" Hay Chettan, (Means elder brother) did you go for a film yesterday without me?" Martin asked with a little resentment : Usually the two brothers go together for movies.

"Yeh. You were busy yesterday night at wharf with your shipment. I got bored sitting idle here. So I went." Micheal justified

"Who went with you?"

"None" '

"But there are two counter foils of tickets."

A sudden jolt in Michael's face was visible.

"Oh…that…that was my office staff." Michael stammered and his face became pale.

Martin had been noticing behavioural changes in Michael's attitudes for sometime. Michael who was a less talkative person started to talk more. He started to sing both in room and also while takeing bath. The perpetual gloomy expression on his face had changed to cheery and smiley face always.

Martin remembered what Sobha, the elder daughter of Advocate Sankara Narayan, the house owner had said to him a few days ago.

"Today brother Michael talked to me for a long time. That was the first time he was talking to me looking at my face. He asked me about my studies, and about my dance practices. He praised me for the best performance I had put up in our school anniversary celebrations. I never knew he was present. He said, he came there with his office staff. "

Martin and Sobha were in friendly terms . She was preparing for her SSLC examination SSLC and Martin was giving her coaching in Mathematics in which he was very good.

"Nowadays, brother Michael smiles at me whenever he sees me. Earlier he never used to give his face even when he was passing by." The younger girl Prabha also commented happily.

Martin asked Michael "Chettan, what made you to change your outlook on life and attitude towards others? You appear to be very happy always. Your pessimistic expression and worried look on face also have gone . how? What happened to you?"

Michael looked at his brother for some time and replied."Marty, now what do we have to worry about? Both of us have good income. You are making much more money than I do. We should be happy indeed, No? As Amma had suggested we are saving our salary in banks. We need not send any money to Amma. Her poultry is also going on well. Then what is there to worry about.I am happy."

That was Michael's explanation. Still Martin had some doubts in his mind.

Another day also Michael went for a movie, when Martin was on night duty at wharf. Martin found two counter foils of cinema ticket, lying in the waste basket.

"Yesterday did you go went for a movie, Chettan?"Martin asked.

" Yes…Yes..How did you know?" Michael asked.

"The couter -foils of tickets were lying in our waste basket. Who was with you?"

"Oh… that …that was my office staff.."

This time also Martin noticed a colour change in Michael's face. He decided to find out who the 'office staff' was . He enquired very secretly. When found out the truth, he was shocked and worried.

The so called office staff, was Maggy! An Anglo Indian girl!

She was his office staff. It was true. A stenographer of Govardhan shipping company, where Michael was working.

Martin knew Maggy well. Who did not know Maggy, the head turner beauty of Fort Cochin! She was the main singer in the Anglo India Choir of Fort Cochin Church. Her solo while serving the 'Eucharist' during the Mass was so captivating to all minds.

Her name itself was beautiful. Maggy. It is the abbreviation of Margaret. means a pearl. Yes. She was really a pearl indeed to many, especially for youth of Cochin.

Her physical features were added to her beauty. She was five feet six inches tall and slim with cropped curly hair. On her high heels she looked six feet tall. She always wore a short frock with low cut neck and sleeveless top. A thin   gold chain with a cross locket on her neck was very apt for her. The frilled frock was only up to the knee and exhibited her, chubby calf muscles tightly wrapped In skin coloured stockings. She had a well shaped body with narrow hip and large bosom. She had a pretty face with painted lips and a long lashed blue eyes. But her way of look was sharp and she was tight lipped which always gave an unfriendly and arrogant expression.

She was the only daughter of an aged tailor, who was a widower, staying in a small house with his tailor shop in front, facing the road located at 'Anglo street' junction near Fort Cochin Church. His name was D'cruz, widely known as tailor D'cruz.A few closely associated with him called 'Boozer D'cruz'

Maggy was not friendly with any one. In choir also she was a loner. She had no close friends like other Anglo Indian girls. Her background might have made her a lonely character

It was a surprise to every one in Govardhan shipping Company, when they came to know that Maggy and Michael were in love and they were going to be married shortly.

"Chettan, it surprised me that you are entangled with that Anglo Indian girl" Martin told Michael. That Maggy is surely a beautiful girl. Though bit fashionable, she is very modest. But I don't support this marriage. I don't want my brother to marry an Anglo Indian girl, daughter of a drunken tailor."

Martin's rude comment hurt Michael. He became upset. He never expected such a blunt reaction from his brother.

"Ours is an orthodox Christian family. We have to maintain certain ethics and our tradition. We have some expectations how the bride should be. We can't accept a high heeled fashionable Anglo girl stepping into our family." Martin said.

" Although she looks fashionable, internly she is an innocent soul, loving and very modest."Michael pleaded.

"I don't think so." Martin turned his face and said sharply. "I know the whole story of her family. Her father, that tailor fellow, though he walks around wearing coat, boots and cap always, is a number one drunkard. Her mother was a cook in Naval Canteen. She was brutally murdered at midnight at Fort Cochin sea shore. Why she had been at sea shore at that hour of night with sailors, that everybody knew. I don't like my brother to get into the trap of such people."

"But ….But…Maggy is not   that ….." Michael pleaded again.

"Maybe. But we don't want her in our family." Martin said sharply and authoritatively.

Micahel could not say a word. He went home and openly discussed with his mother Eliamma. But she was biased. She was already briefed by Martin before Michael could talk to mother. Eliamma did not give her consent for the marriage

The reciprocale actions taken by aggravated Michael was heart breaking to Martin. Michael shifted his stay from Advocate Sankara Narayanan's house to Maggy's house, leaving his brother alone. It was a big blow to Martin. That was not expected at all.

"My brother Martin has grown more than me. He is capable and strong. Stronger than me. It is better to part." That was what Michael had said to the Advocate, the house owner, before he left the house with his belongings and settled his rent. Martin was not present when he left. He was at wharf with his shipment works.

Martin felt upset and lonely in the world. He never expected that his loving brother would go away leaving him alone. He was not only his brother, he was his protector, guide, friend and all. He felt it difficult to live in that house without Michael. He cried throughout the night, gripping and embracing the pillow on which his brother was resting his head when sleeping. Next day he took leave and brooded in the room thinking what to do next. He should not have talked to his brother in such a rude way. It he loves that girl, why should he object? If his love towards her was so deep, which changed his attitudes and life style,and also she succeeded in making him a social man.

He wanted to talk to his brother. He wanted to appologize him for his rude words and bring him back to the house. Before that he wanted to talk to his mother Eliamma. It is me who had induced defiance and objection in her.   He rushed to his house at Mundalam, Pala. The whole day they were talking only about Michael. Eliamma accused Martin for talking in rude manner to his elder brother.

" If he likes that girl so much, we will get them married in our Mundalam Church The new Vicar Fr. Raphel is a very realistic and very social person. He always talks about the amity and harmony amongst the people, family and Churches. Schism is not at all in line with the Christian doctrine, he always preaches. I don't think he will object this marriage, just because the girl is from Anglo Indian community and Latin Rite."

Eliamma gave her consent for the marriage.

Martin had to   stay two weeks at Mundalam with his mother as they had planned to renovate the house. He had sufficient money in his bank account for the renovation. He had to call the contractor, chalked out the plan and awarded the contract.

Martin made another mistake of not consulting with his brother on the renovation of their house. Eliamma also did not think of it. They thought what ever they do would be acceptable to Michael too. That was their line of thinking

When Martin reached Cochin after two weeks, his immediate agenda was to meet his brother and convey the happy news about the consent of their mother for the marriage. But he was welcomed with a shocking news of Michal's marriage which was scheduled to be held on that day at ten O clock at Fort Cochin Church!

"Didn't he tell you, about his marriage.? What an idiot he is. He should have taken the blessings from his mother." Advocate Sankara Narayan told Martin.

"I will be attending the wedding feast. I have an invitation It is at 11 o clock."

" It is all my mistake." Martin cursed himself and looked at the watch. It was already ten!

He rushed to ' Cherlai flower market" on his bicycle, bought a small flower bouquet and padalled fast to Fort Cochin church.

The entire Anglo Indian community was at the entrance of the church which indicated the marriage was already solemnised. All gentlemen gathered were in their best suits. That was the Anglo Indian tradition. Even a begger, if he belonged to Anglo Indian community, would wear a suit to attend a marriage . Ladies would be in their best frocks, and would have beautiful head dresses or hats. Their faces would be over made up and lip sticked in thick red.

Martin felt about himselfan odd man out in his pants and slacks. He had not worn his shoes. Only sandals which was considered to be indecent for Anglo Indians

He waited away from the crowd, with the bouquet in his hand, for the bride and groom to come out of the church.

His waiting was long. Finally they came out, the bride and groom! Michael looked like a film star in his dark blue new suits. Martin was seeing his brother in suits for the first time. Maggy was in her white long wedding gown. The crown and long veil fitted on her head had given her the look   of a princess, and she looked beautiful. A cameraman was running around the couple and catching their different angles with his heavy camera.   All were looking at them with smile and happy faces.

Maggy saw Martin standing at a distance alone holding the bouquet in his   hands.   She   shouted   very   loudly   with   all   her might."Hay…Marty…….."

All the feelings and emotions upsurged in her reflected in her loud shrill voice. Her sound echoed in the compound of the church . All turned their heads and looked at Martin. Maggy lifted her hand and beckoned Martin to come fast and closer

Martin walked very reluctantly towards the couples . Michael turned his face in disgust and disgrace.

Maggy took the bouquet from his hand, kissed it, and gave it to Michael. He took it in bewilderment.

"Thank You Maggy" Martin said

Call me chechy now onwards. I am your chechi. Only chechi" she said with an affectionate smile (Chechi means elder sister)

She put her right hand over the shoulder of Martin, with left arm she circled Michael's arm and paused for photos, when the crowd was applauding.

Martin was overwhelmed and he felt like crying. He looked at his brother Michael. He was also crying then, silently.

CHAPTER 13

TRAGEDY IN MANA

Advocate Sankara Narayanan, the house owner was one of the guests for Michael's marriage, and for the feast after the wedding. The entire office staff of Govardhan Shipping company, where Micheal and Maggy were working, also were invited. The feast was arranged in the parish hall and the food was seved in British style, buffet.

The Anglo Indians at Cochin, were very fond of British systems and customs. Whatever they do, it would be done only in British style.

The term 'Anglo Indian' is referred to two groups. One, those with mixed Indian and British ancestry and the other is original British descent born or living permanently in India. Cochin group was the former type. But most of them were pretended to belong to the second group. Maggy's father, D'cruz was one among them.

But, Maggy was different. Though always she always dressed herself in frocks and wore high heel shoes, she adored Indian culture. She was proud to be an Indian, but people thought otherwise, because of her dressing

"I will not attend the feast as our mother was not invited. Neither me. You should be ashamed of it, chettan." Martin said to Michael, and walked towards the gate swiftly.

It was a great blow to Michael.

Maggy became upset for a   while. Her face saddened, eyes filled and two drops of tears fell through her cheeks.

Immediately after the wedding function the first thing Maggy asked to Michael was to take her to his Mother at Mundalam, Pala, to ask apology and seek blessings.

Michael was embarrassed, and felt distressed. But he had to oblige as Maggy was adamant. They proceeded to Pala by a taxi car. When they reached Mundalam, Pala, it was midnight and Eliamma was fast asleep. They had to wake her up. Eliamma was astonished when she saw his son Michael and his bride right in front of her at that hour of night. That was not expected at all.

Maggy knelt before the mother and   touched her feet with great reverence.

"Bless me mother" Maggy said in sob.

Eliamma was stunned. She made her to get up by holding both her shoulders and embraced the bride with a lot of affection and love. She kissed her both cheecks. Whatever sadness and apprehensions she had in her mind had been swiped out by the tears of her daughter in law.

"Let me see closely my son's bride, my dear daughter in law."

Eliamma brightened the hurricane lamp and held closely to Maggy. She viewed her from tip to toe very eagerly.

She was astonished again. Because she expected a modern lady in an Anglo Indian costume. But what she saw in front of her was a beautiful modest angel looking girl wearing the traditional dress of Kerala women, the 'Set mundu' and blouse.

Set Mundu consist of long cloth around the waist and half saree over it. Both would have guilt boarder.

"Hay, you look wonderfull..." Eliamma exclaimed happily." Our bride is beautiful"

Michael and Maggy stayed with mother for three days at Manassery house.

"Daughter Maggy, my son Michael is not that proactive, as my other son Martin. His actions are always delayed and untimely. You have to guide him." Eliamma advised her daughter in law.

 She wrote to Martin about Maggy. "A Laxmi has come to our home." Laxmi is the Hindu Goddess of wealth, fortune and prosperity.

****

That was Sunday and Martin had a relaxed day. He was about to go out to have his dinner from a nearby Brahmin's hotel. The time was eight at night.

Advocate Sankara Narayanan, knocked the door and entered the room unexpectedly. He was looking very tired and worried.   Climbing the stairs was a strain for him. He was panting heavily .

"Kindly be seated sir." Martin invited him to a chair.

"I thought of having a personal chat with you. That's why I climbed those stairs ".

" I know you are sick for sometime. But don't know exactly what is the problem. Sobha told me it is some sort of ulcer or something like that."

"Even I do not know what was my actual problem. I was taking a lot of medicines. But all those were wrong medicines. Only yesterday my actual problem was diagnosed. Dr. Menon, the new Physician in our Govt. Hospital told me yesterday that I am having an acute cirrhosis. My liver has already been completely damaged, and a recovery would not be possible."

"But sir, you are a teetotaler. How that could be. Cirrhosis is a disease of drunkards."

"Usually yes. It also can happen by the reactions of some medicines. I was taking a lot of Ayurvedic medicines from my youth, to improve my health. 'Lehiyam,' 'Arishtam', etc. They all contained a lot of ingredients which had an adverse effect on my liver, That's what doctor suspects. well,   I have come to you now to discuss about another matter."

"Tell me sir."

" You have been in my house for the last three years."

"Yes sir"

"Yes . true. Initially I was collecting from you and Michael only five rupees as rent. I would have asked more. But your condition was very pathetic. Last year I was compelled to hike the rent to rupees ten each. You know, Martin, I can easily get minimum forty rupees if I give this house to a family. But what I get from you is only twenty rupees. Now, Michael has gone, and what I will get from you is only ten rupees. See, I am sick. I have no savings and do not have any other income either. You don't know how much strain I am taking to meet both the ends. Now, as you know, Sobha passed SSLC with good marks and she has got admission in Maharajas College on merit basis. Next Monday we have to remit one hundred and fifty rupees in the college. I don't have any money to give her. I don't know what to do? " Sankara Narayanan looked very upset. He sat silently for some time.

"Sir, ,what do you want me to do?" Martin asked.

"I want you to find out another place and vacate this house at the earlist, so that I can give this house to some family. Your brother Michael is staying at Fort in that Anglo Indian Colony. You can go and stay with him." Sankara Narayanan suggested.

Martin was shocked. But he did not express it on his face.

"Do you want me to pay you more?"

"No   Martin. How much more would you be able to give?. There is a limit, is int' it? Better you shift the house, so that I can accommodate a family at higher rent. It would be   a great help." The old man was pleading.

"How much are you expecting from a family tenant.?"Martin asked.

"At least forty. I will ask for fifty."

"This   month onwards I will give you fifty rupees per month. I want to stay here. I won't get a homely atmosphere like here anywhere else. I love your family. I   love Ammai like my mother." Martin said and what he said was true.

Sankara Narayanan looked at him with respect.

"Brunton Company is paying you well, is in't it?" He asked

"Not bad, I am doing a lot of overtime work."

"You are working hard."

"Getting opportunity to work itself is a grace."

"That 's a great thinking. God will bless you my son. I don't have a son like you, Martin." The old man's throat chocked with emotion. His eyes became moistured.

"Son , may I ask you another favour?"

"Tell me sir."

"Can you give me a loan of one hundred and fifty rupees by next Monday. I don't have money to give to Sobha for her college admission." He asked with lot of delicacy.

"No problem sir, It would be arranged. Now you go peacefully."

"Martin, you are like my son. I wanted to reveal my mental agony to some one. That's why I am telling you. I don't have much time left. My liver is completely gone. There is no recovery possible. That's what Dr. Menon told. Remedy is transplantation of liver. That facility is not available in Kerala. Only in Bombay, and that will cost thousands. It will not be possible for a poor man like me. If I happened to die, Bhageerathy would not have any money with her even to do my cremation…" He could not complete his words. A sob was heard near the half closed door. Martin and Sankara Narayanan looked up. Bhagerathy Amma was standing behind the door. She was whimpering. "Oh…Bhagy, you were standing there.?" Sankara Narayan asked in wonder with trembling voice.

"You never told me about your disease. I heard everything that you said." She cried.

"Bhagy, I also came to know the details only two days back."

Sankara Narayanan got up, bid farewell to Martin with gesture and walked towards the door. He caught hold of the hand of his wife and stepped down the staircase very slowly and carefully. Martin looked at them with sympathy.

At midnight, a loud cry was heard, and Martin jumped out of his bed. He was fast asleep. He thought it was the hauling of stray dogs in the street. But he heard his name was called out loudly and it was Sobha's sound.

He ran down the stairs, and rushed to the house. The front door was closed. The screaming of ladies was   heard from inside. He banged the door and Prabha opened the door, crying.

The sight was horrible and fearful. Sankarana Narayanan was lying flat on the floor in a pool of   blood. His mouth was widly open. Blood was oozing out through the   corner of his   mouth. Ladies were yelling hysterically.

"Hold yourself Sobha. This is the time we have to act quickly . Stop crying and clean his face with a wet towel. I will run and get a cycle rickshaw." Having said this, he ran out.

As usual, there were two cycle rikshaws parked at the junction, near Amman coil temple. Both the riksha workers were sleeping in their rikshaws squeezed themselves into the passengers seat.

Martin tapped them to wake up.

"Hurry, both   of you, we have to rush to the hospital with a patient. It is an emergency." Martin said hurriedly loudly.

"Fare is two rupees each sir." The rikshaw man demanded, exploiting the emergency.

"Oh..that's all right. Let us move and pedal." Within ten minutes both the rikshaws reached at the gate of ' Mana'

With the help of the rickshawalas, Martin lifted Sankara Narayanan and   made him   to lie on the passengers seat, his legs genuflected. Martin sat on its foot resting platform holding Sankara Narayanan, firmly.

"You   follow in the other riksha." He told Sobha.

They could reach hospital within thirty minutes. But by the time Advocate Sankara Narayanan was dead.

CHAPTER 14

BUDDING OF LOVE

Even a minute's change in nature will have its reciprocation on lives on earth. But even great occurrences in lives would never make any impact on nature.

Advocate Sankara Narayanan was dead and burned into ashes in the municipal crematorium. Even the remembrance of him would be eroded from the mind of his fellowmen in due course of time.

That day also the sun rose and set as usual. Breeze has flown normally. Birds sang and flew as ever before.

That was also another usual day for Martin. But the death of Sankara Narayanan has changed his routines and the way of life. That change made him distinctly different.

Earlier, Martin was having his food alone, from different hotels. That was changed to eating of homemade food prepared and served by Bhagerathy Amma and dined along with Sobha and Prabha in their dining room at 'Mana'. In return Martin was repaying their debts at provision shop and vegetable shop. Situations compelled   him to pay off all other debts too. Gradually he became the house holder of 'Mana'.

Sobha did not take the admission in the college. She dropped the idea of higher studies. She took a job as a Dance teacher in 'Brahmin's Dance School" at Mattanchery near Boat Jetty, just behind the Mattanchery Palace.

Daily morning Martin used to drop her at dance school on his bicycle, on route to his office at Willingdon Island. He was using the ferry service to go to Island. He was entitled for an annual ferry pass for him and for his cycle, arranged by his Company.

Cycle riding with girls by the youth was not a big issue in Cochin. It was common to see, youngsters, riding their bicycles with their girlfriends sitting on the cross bars of their cycles. Cochi was known as lovers paradise. Later, Municipality banned the 'over load' on the city roads.

Bhageerathy Amma did not raise any objection for Sobha to go with Martin on his bicycle, as she could save two kilometer walking alone. However, there was a burning sensation in her heart whenever she saw both of them were riding like love birds on public roads.

She remembered her younger age, about twenty years ago. She was in love with her neighbour, young advocate Sankaran . Sankaran has just started his practice at Mattanchery   Munsif Court, situated at 'Pyari' Junction and she was learning type writing in an institute near the Court. Every morning they were going together from house by walk. It was three kilometers walk from Palluruthy , where their houses were situated.

Bhageerathy belonged to 'Mullackal' an ancient orthodox Nair family and Sankaran was from EzhavaThoppil family.   Narayanan, father of Sankaran was a labourer at 'Mullackal' family. He had a chance to go to Malaysia, along with a few other labourers in a country craft to work in Rubber plantations. He could earn a lot of money and come back to his native village after few years, as a rich man.

Meantime, Mullackal family was in its decay due to a lot of litigations and liqudations. Narayanan could acquire a major portion of Mullackal property, which was under auction by court orders. Acquiring of property by someone who was once their labourerer, had become a prestige issue for Mullackal people and they considered it as an indignity to them.

Both the families became sworn enemies. Even for a silly boundary dispute, Krishnan Nair (Bhagerathy's father) had a big fight with Narayanan, which resulted in the murder of the former. It was not a deliberate homicide. It was accidental. As a requital, Narayanan and his wife, the Parents of Sankaran were brutally killed by the brothers of Bhageerathy and they   were jailed.

Young advocate Sankaran fled from the native Palluruthy, to Cochin with his lover Bhageerathy, who happened to be pregnant at that time. They wanted a

hide out urgently. Sankaran's advocate friends found a house for them at Fort Cochin   near Amman coil. That was a 'Mana' that belonged to a 'Kongini' which was under liquidation. With the help of a Court order they purchased the house and registered the deed in Sankaran's name at a cost of Five hundred and fifty rupees. ('Mana' means typical Brahmins house) . This was in the year 1939.

It was a big money in those days.When one 'Idangazi' rice (approximatedly one kilo) had only one 'chakram' (local coin) which was equivalent to $1/28^{th}$ of a rupee. Gold sovereign was costing only three rupees (eight gram)

Advocate Sankaran had to borrow one hundred rupees on interest from

a pawn broker by name Sait for the purchase of the 'Mana'

Sankaran and his wife Bhageerathy never had any contact with their

families thereafter. Even for the funeral of Sankara Narayanan, none of

their relatives attended, either.

Sankaran was an honest man. He had true love for Bhageerathy. "Does

Martin have the same honesty and true love for Sobha?" Bhageerathy

was afraid.

"Son, Martin, we have none in this world to protect us or to help us."

One day Bageerathy Amma told Martin, when he was having food with

her daughters. She wanted to tell him all her apprehensions, she has

been

suppressing   in her mind. But, looking at his face she forgot whatever

she was planning to tell him.

"When God is with us, why worry for not having others with you?"

Martin asked. "Same way what is the use when all are with you, but

God?"

That was his belief too. But that was not the answer Bageerathy Amma expected from him. She wanted an assurance from him that he would never leave them.

That was supposed to be a busy day for Martin. There was loading on more ships. He thought of going to wharf early.

But he got up little late on that day. Hurriedly he jumped out of the bed, and as usual, he opened the door, stood at balcony for a while, and took long breaths. Surveyed the surroundings lazily, looked at the horizon and prayed. His prayer was brief and short.

"Oh God. Thank you for everything. Bless me to do everything in its right way"

He rushed to the toilet after stripping his clothes on the way and put it on the bed, He took a towel from the cloth hanger, entered into bath room and shut its door.

The water was very cold. He finished his wash and bath swiftly and came out of the bath room naked, by drying his hair.

He was shocked in horror on seeing Sobha standing right in front of him, holding 'prasad' from temple (blessed sandal paste in a piece of plantain leaf)

He never knew that she had entered the room.

"Hay you! " He exclaimed very loudly and frighteningly. Immediately he tried to wrap the towel around his waist. But it was too short for his waist. He ran and picked up his long cloth from the bed and wore it quickly.

Sobha laughed aloud as if she had seen a fun.

"What the hell are you doing here, at this hour? Why didn't you knock? Don't you know that this is a bachelor's room? " Martin barked.

 She continued laughing hysterically and said" Sorry…..Sorry"

"What sorry? Now stop this bloody laughing."

His face was furious and sound was arrogant.

"I said sorry Marty…" she said pleading.

"OK….OK.. That's alright. I thought I will have a heart attack due to the shock. What made you to come in now.?"

"You know the importance of this day."

"You have seen me naked?"

"Not that. To day is your birth day."

"Oh…that's it. I have forgotten that. Even otherwise who cares about birthdays. That's all for kids. I am a grown up man."

"Yes . you are a grown up man, that I have seen." She laughed again.

"Oh..stop it. Let us not talk about it."

" I went to temple, offered a "Pushpanjaly" (Offering of flowers) and prayed for you."

She took a little sandal paste on her fingers from the Plantain leaf fold and applied it on his forehead.

"Thanks." Martin said smilingly.

"I brought another gift for you."

"What is it?"

"Close your eyes a while"

He closed his eyes.

Suddenly Sobha embarraced him by holding him tightly and kissed him on his lips. The warmth of her fleshly bosom and the fragrance from her curly hair sent hot waves through his nerves. His entire body was horripilation.

He could not control himself. He pulled and embraced, pressed her tightly against his chest. They lost themselves into an unknown fantasy and fell on the bed, panting heavely.

CHAPTER 15

BACKLASH BY GOD

That was December eighth, the festival day for Catholic, in commemoration of Immaculate Conception of Mother Mary, the Mother of Jesus. Christians all over the world celebrate that auspicious day. A colourful procession carrying the idol of Mother Mary on a well decorated chariot would be the ceremonial event. Some churches would conduct candle light processions at night.

In Vatican, St. Peters Basilica also celebrates that day with a Pontifical Mass led by Pope at St. Peters Square, immediately after the Papal Audience.

St. Peter's square is the pride of Vatican, situated in front of St. Peters Basilica . Vatican is the smallest independent nation, located within the city of Rome in Italy, having an extent of one hundred and ten acres only, out of which twenty acres are utilised for St. Peters square. Eighty thousand people could be assembled there, including twenty thousand seats. Chairs could be booked in advance, to witness the Papal audience and open air Holy Mass by Pope. On all Wednesdays and a few selected holidays, Pope would pass through the crowd in an open jeep, escorted by cardinals and Swiss guards to give Apostolic blessings to the people. The crowd would greet the Pope by cheering with Viva il Papa, Viva il Papa "jubilation. The entire Vatican would vibrate by the shouts of people Thousands of pilgrims reach Vatican on all the Public Audience days to receive the Apostolic blessings from Pope.

It is worth studying the management system of bus parking near St. Peter's Square, where thousands of tourist buses from different countries were parked in lines and rows.

That day a tourist group from Pala, Kerala, reached Vatican. They had visited different pilgrim centres and their last visiting station was Vatican.

Father Zacharias was among them.

It was his long cherished desire to visit Vatican and see the Pope, personally. He was very eager to see St. Peter's Basilica, the capital of all Churches in the world. He was mobilizing funds for quite some time for the purpose. He did pay eighteen thousand rupees for his journey expenditure including air ticket. And that was a big amount in those days.

Fr.Zacharias was transferred from Mundalam church to Pala Bishops palace, and was assigned with some liturgical responsibilities.

After visiting the 'Sistine Chapel' where the election of Pope used to take place, the Vatican Musium, Art gallery and the underground cemetery where the holy tombs of St. Peter and other saints were situated, the group reached St. Peter's square to attend the Papal Audience and the Holy Mass by Pope.

Fr. Zacharias was astonished to see the huge crowd at St peter's Square. He could get a comfortable seat about fifty yards (feet) away from the Altar. Zacharias was so thrilled to be there and was very contented and blissful.

It was ten O' clock in the morning. The bells on the tower of St.Peters Baslica started to swing swiftly, ringing aloud. Usually bells would be steady and its tongue would swing to ring. In St. Peter's Beslica it was the other way round. The tongue would be steady and the bells swing. It was wonderful to watch. Band music was heard loudly through high powered speakers fitted around the square.

A loud applause was heard. Pope John the Twenty Third, appeared standing on a jeep with his extended hands, accompanied by two

Cardinals and escorted by Swiss guards. The jeep was moving into the crowd, but through pre determined barricaded passage, guarded by Italian police. The crowd   greeted the Pope with loud cheers. Fr. Zacharia also shouted with all his might "Viva il Papa" and waved both his hands to greet the Holy Father.

He could see the Pope, very closely at twenty feet away. He felt, Pope had looked at him and waved his hand on him. Almost everyone in the crowd had the same feeling. When Pope had withdrawn and disappeared, St. Peters Square became silent.

Then it was time for Holy Mass. Again the bells started to swing and ring loudly. Music was heard. Pope appeared on the altar led by a procession of twelve 'Deacons' dressed in Red and white garments. The Deacon in front was holding the "Papal Cross." Behind him, there were ten Deacons in two lines with folded hands. The twelfth Deacon, a black skinned man, was holding the Holy Bible, and he was walking just in front of the Pontiff. The Pope was in his ceremonial Mass attire with the Papal regalia and insignia, "the big keys and crown" embroided on the chest.   Three Cardinals were walking behind. It was a majestic show.

" Nel nome del padre e del figlio e dello spirito santo!!" (In the name of the father , and of the son and of the Holy Spirit)

Mass started with a prayer by Pope.

The crowd replied, "Amen"

The Mass proceeded, and it was time for Liturgy of the word. The black skinned Deacon took the Bible from the Altar and knelt before the Pope. The Pontiff blessed him by keeping his hand on his head and allowed him to kiss the "Fisher man's Ring" that he worn on his finger.

The Deacon came forward and stood on a podium. The entire crowd was looking at him. Zacharias felt a familiarity on that face. He continued to stare at him, with a suspicion in his mind.

The Deacon adjusted the microphone and announced loudly in Italian language. "Prima Lettura" meaning ' First reading."

His voice was very clear and throaty. He opened the Bible and started to read. "Leggendo del libro di Esodo" meaning "Reading   from the book of Exodus.

A chill passed through the nerves of Fr. Zacharias. He could recollect and recognise that voice. It was the same harsh voice that was heard during funerals at Mundalam cemetery, while coffins were descented into the grave;the instructions of the grave digger!

He looked at the face of Deacon very carefully. A doubt bounced in his mind.

He recognised the face! Yes! It was Ouseph!! The son of grave digger Pathrose, who used to take lead to bury the coffins, in the absence of his father. The same Ouseph, who was denied by him entry to Mundalam Church Altar. Now he is on the Altar of St. Peters Basilica, assisting the Mass of Pope, the Holy Father!

Fr. Zacharias started to sweat. His inner clothes were drenched in sweat. The atmospheric temperature at Vatican was ten degrees at that time. A cold wave also was blowing to make every one sitting in open air to shiver. Yet Zacharias was sweating.

He gripped his chair firmly and tried to hold himself from falling. But his eyes became blurred and he could not hold further. He collapsed and fell on the ground. His companions, and fellow tourists picked him up and made him to sit on the chair. Someone sprinkled water on his face and gave him a bottle of water to drink.   He drank the full bottle in one go.

" What happened father? " One man asked.

I saw Jesus... I   saw Jesus" Zacharias said with a shivering voice, as if he was in somnambulism.

Weeks passed by. Christmas and New year also went by as usual. Europe was in the grip of into bitter cold, and the temperature, touched minus ten degrees   at night. There was thick fog everywhere, reducing the visibility to a few feet. People longed for sunlight.

Pope's speech to Aspirants of SDA seminary, once in a month was in their faculty schedule. Usually the speech would be for one hour. On that day the Pope talked only fifteen minutes. . He looked very tired and sick.

It was rumoured that the Pontif was infected with cancer.

On that day the Pope concluded his speech by stressing the importance of prayer. Pope said. "The ways and means of Providence is unknown to man. If anyone tells that he had the vision of Gods will, he is telling lie. He is telling his own imagination. However, we can take God's guidance through meditation and by deep prayers. At that time also what upsurges in our mind need not be God's will or guidance. It could be from Satan too. To distinguish God's direction and that of

Satan, we must have His Grace. To get his Grace one should go into deep prayers. Even Jesus was practicing deep prayer to overcome Satan. That's why Jesus advised us to pray hard and continuously to get away from temptations. "

It was dark when Ouseph reached his hostel after the class by Pope. A big envelop was waiting for him on his bed. His heart jumped with joy. The letter was from Martin.

He tore open the envelop. There was a greeting card and a sheet of paper written on both sides.

Martin wrote."May I start this letter with sad news. Fr. Zacharias who was the Vicar of Mundalam Catholic Church, had passes away a few days back.

I met him a few weeks ago at Cochin Airport. I was there at Cargo department taking delivery of a consignment of my company.

I saw Fr. Zacharias coming out of Bombay flight. I went to him to greet. Afterall he was our Vicar and from our place. He was looking tired and sick . He was coming back after a European tour . He told me that he was at Vatican and saw you on the altar assisting Pope's Mass.

He told me to write to you to   pardon him for the way he was treating you.

He is dead now.   He was infected with pneumonia. Ouseph, please don't keep any grudge on that old man. "

Ouseph felt shocked.

He ran to the Chapel to pray for Fr. Zacharias.

CHAPTER 16

SACRUM HIT

Greek merchant ship "SS.PAVIS" was one of the regular visiting ships at Cochin Port. She was on sail between Europe and India and used toberth at Cochi Port bimonthly. Brunton Company was her agent in India. 'PAVIS' was stuck at Cochin port for ten days due to an unexpected labour strike, and loading and unloading were delayed. When the strike was called off, the Captain made a hue and cry to sail out the ship. He wanted to leave the port before midnight, as metrological department had broadcast a serious weather warning, a storm at Mali sector. Before the storm struck, Captain wanted to cross the Mali Cape.

To add to his fury, the 'Ship stores supplier, ' the famous ' Chandler' Mohammed Koya had delayed to deliver the kitchen stores. Without stocking the' ship stores' for thirty days, it was impossible for him to sail out the ship.

A shocking news was received then, that the Chandalier had met with an accident. The Chandler Mohammed Koya, while on his way to wharf with the stores, his truck had collided with a lorry at Broadway,

Ernakulam. His truck was overturned and the entire load, including fresh meet, fish and other perishable stuff were scattered on the road, resulting a heavy traffic block. The driver of the truck died on the spot. The Chandler Mohammed Koya who was sitting by the side of the driver was seriously injured. He was taken to Ernakulam General Hospital and his condition was critical. He was also said to be dead.

"I don't bother about the death of the stores supplier. Please find out another "Chandler" immediately and get me the ship stores. I want to sail out the ship before midnight at any cost. Please do something. I can't sail without kitchen stores stocked full." The captain barked at Martin, who was the representative of the ship agent, Broutan Company.

Both Captain and Martin were standing near taffsail of the deck of 'Pavis' ship.

" Sir, it is not that easy to locate a licensed Chandler at this hour. There are only three or four people who supply meat and fish to ships. They would be in the market now, busy in buying the store items for other ships." Martin expressed his inability.

"Then you go and buy the stores for us." Captain suggested.

" Me..? I am an officer of Brunton Company, your steamer agents. I am not a Chandlier." Martin said with an irritation.

Chandler business, supplying of kiitchen items particularly fresh meat and fish to ships was considered to be a job of lower dignity. But its hidden benefits were unknown to Martin.

"My dear, young man, don't think, Chandler job is an inferior work. Purchasing of food items is superior to any other job. When I am at home I do all the shopping. You are smart and young. You represent our Agent Company and you have the moral obligation to meet our needs. You are a native of this town and you know the market places well. Please hire a vehicle, go to shops and purchase all our items immediately. So that I can sail out today. Please."

"Sir, to supply stores to ship a Chandler license is required. I don't have one."

" Of course, I know that. Let us go to customs and get a temporary licence for you. I will come with you and explain the Customs Superintendent the emergency situation we are in. "

Fortunately, at that moment, Martin saw, the customs superintendent Mr. Kesavan passing through the 'shore jetty' along with a few uniformed preventive officers. They were on their routine inspection round.

"Sir, here he is. The man in civil dress coming along with the Custom's Officers is Mr. Kesavan, the Customs Superintendent."

The Captain ran down the ramp from the ship to dock and called loudly. "Sir….Sir…"
 His voice was frantic.

The customs officers were stunned to see the gigantic figure of a European running towards them. They talked for some time while Martin was watching from the ship deck.

Immediately an order was issued by the Superintendent of Customs to issue a temporary Chandler License" to Martin of Brunton Company, to supply ship stores to "S.S Pavis' only."
"What are the items you want me to purchase? I don't have money to buy them for you." Martin said.
Usually, the Chandlers were used to   invest money in advance to procure the items, submit the bill to Captain and get the money. That was the procedure.
"Don't bother about money" captain said.

He gave him a list of the items to be purchased. He also gave the quotation submitted by Mohammed Koya earlier.

Ship stores were supplied against the approved quotation submitted by the Chandler.

Martin went through the list. There were sixty items. Grocery, provisions, cereals, oils, vegetables, fruits, meat, fish , detergents and cosmetics were in the list. When he glanced through the approved quotation, Martin was shocked. He could not believe his eyes! Cost of beef which was only two rupees per kilo in the market, quoted by Mohammed Koya was, Two Dollars per Kilo!

The Exchange rate of dollar was twenty seven dollar per rupee at that time in 1964. The Chandler was supplying the beef to the ship at a rate of fifty four rupees per kilo! It was unbelievable. Likewise were all the items. Commodity   costing one rupee was quoted for one dollar!

Captain said." I know, the prevailing market rates are high. But Mohammed Koya was supplying us at old rates. And we were very thankful to him. Please try to maintain the same rates if you can. Slight escalation if deemed necessary can be acceptable. No problem. "

Martin did not make any comment. He stood stunned in front of Captain.

By giving money to Martin, the captain said. "Martin Sir, Mohammed Koya was supplying me a secret item which is not written in the list. I can't write it. I don t know whether you will be able to supply me that item. "

" What is that ? Drugs ? No. that I can't ."

"No Martin. I don't take drugs, and I don't allow my crew also to use it either. I want arrack. It is very common here, and sold it in public No.?"

"Of course, arrack is not prohibited here."

"But the customs won't allow you to bring that stuff to ship. If found they will confiscate and you will be fined. You may have to hide it in the vegetable bags. "

" How many bottles do you want? "

"Four bottles. Mohammed Koya told me, there are two types of arrack available. One is first quality and the other is second quality . I want only first quality, though prize is bit high. He was charging me five dollars per first quality bottle. I like its flavor. It is distilled from

Coconut toddy, is in't it? It is far better than Russian Vodka, and Chinese Shaojin." Captain laughed.

"I don't know about it. I don't take arrack."

"Good, don't take it. It is not good for youth. It would weaken your erotic power." Captain laughed loudly.

Martin remembered the price list of arrack,   that was hung in front of the arrack shop at Cherlai junction. "arrack full Bottle– Rs. 3/-,Half Bottle   -
Rs. 2/- , Quarter bottle = Rs.   1/-" He knew there were no different qualities either. That was Mohammed Koya's marketing stunt.

Captain gave Martin Four Five doller notes and said." This is for arrack, for four bottles. This is for my personall use."

He further, gave ten one hundred dollar notes separately and said ." This is thousand dollar, for our stores supply. Please give me proper bill neatly written in white paper. "

Martin knew he hit a gold mine. In that deal what Martin earned was fifteen thousand rupees and that was a very huge money in those days.

Martin obtained a 'Permanent chandler licence' from customs on his name. His application for the licence was forwarded by Brunton company to effect 'stores supply ' to the ships under their agency . But Martin was supplying stores to all the ships berthed or   moored at Cochin Port.

A new life was opened for Martin. His growth was immense and it was beyond his imaginations.

In all his further growth, the involvement of Hamza Mooppan was very prominent. Hamza Mooppan was the labour gang leader (Mooppan), hence the name. Hamza was about fifty years of age with very good physique. He was addressing Martin as 'Sir' and he liked the young man from the very   first day of their meeting.

Hamza was a known wrestler,   with thorough knowledge on vital nerve points of human anatomy. He was utilizing this secret knowledge while   wrestling or fighting, to win over his opponent. He was specialized in a vulnerable Arabic stunt tactic called "Sacrum hit," learned from Saudi Arabia when he was working their as a labourer.

"Sacrum hit" was a very dangerous fighting tactic. Lift the opponent high above the head, by holding his thigh with one hand and gripping on his neck   by the other hand and then hit the opponant on the ground hard by his sacrum. His spinal cord would be shaken and hip bone would be cracked. The victim had to be hospitalized minimum for six months.

There were many who had experienced the misery of Hamza's 'sacrum hit'. People were afraid of that gigantic man. The association with Hamza had changed the course of direction of Martin's life. He started growing financially and his reputation spread over the area.

CHAPTER 17

OSARIO DUKDOM

That was 3rd June, 1963.Pope John XXIII, who was the Sovereign of Vatican City state, passed away. He was 81.

His original name before becoming Pope was ' Angelo Giuseppe Roncalli, in short "Roncalli". He was the fourth of fourteen children born to a peasant family of Lombardy village, Italy. He ruled Vatican and Catholic Church for a period of Five years. He was bed ridden for seven months of abdominal cancer.

It was a big lose to Catholic Church, and it was a great lose to Ouseph personally.   The name change from Ouseph to Ouso was made by Pope as a honour for his passing of novitiate at first chance and getting his batchlor's degree from 'University of Rome ' by Correspondence Course . Pope was very much pleased with Deacon Ouso.

The Pontiff had a special interest in Deacon Ouso. Pope wanted him to become an ideal priest, as he learned his track record from the file, submitted by the Rector of seminary, along with his confidential report on him. Ouseph was the only person to reach Seminary from socially downtrodden life. Pope was moved by knowing the life story of Ouseph.

Pope made him his 'Personal Orderly And Aid' (POA). Ouseph was often seen standing behind Pope, whenever he had appeared in public functions. The face of Deacon Ouseph became very familiar to Vatican and everybody respected him.

There was a saying among the senior priests that Deacon Ouso was likely to become a Pope in future, or at least a Cardinal, as it was the case of Pope John himself. When Pope John was a Deacon he was POA to Pope Pius X during 1903 – 1914, who became a saint. The seniors observed many similarities between Ouso and Angelo Roncalli, except the skin colour issue. But God looks at the soul and not at the skin, which would be decomposed and be turned into dust in the grave.

When Pope John became sick and bedridden, Monsignor Dr.Michaclosky was assigned to take care of his treatment and personal care. There was a panel of allopathy doctors and nurses who were working under the old man Monsignor Michaelasky. Both the Pope and Michaelosky were buddies when they were young. Both were of same age, 81 Michaelosky was a known Homeo Doctor.

During world war I, Fr. Angelo Roncalli and Fr. Michaelosky were drafted into Italian Army in the ranks of sergeants, serving in Medical corp as 'stretcher - bearers'. Later both became Army Chaplains.

Though the Pope was under allopathic treatment, Michaelosky was parallely administering Homeo Medicines to Pope, which gave him smooth sedation and comfortable sleep . That was what Michaelosky intended too.

Deacon Ouso was deputed to assist Michaelosky. He was chosen by Pope himself. Ouso has always been at Pope's room along with Michaelosky. He was present when Pope had his last breath.

There were two great ceremonial functions held at St. Peter's square on March 3rd and June 21st in 1963, in which, the State heads of all nations and millions of people gathered. June 3rd was the funeral ceremony of Pope John XXIII, and June 21st was 'Papal Coronation' of Pope Paul VI. "Papal Coronation" was the ceremony of placing the 'Papal Tiara' on the head of the newly elected Pope: 'Papal Tiara' is a three – tired gold crown, with many precious stones on it. Tiara was meritorious and highly valued. Such crown was worn by Popes from as early as 8th century. Pope Paul VI abandoned the coronation of Tiara during his

Papacy, as he felt that it was too much of a luxury and not suitable for the follower of ' Big Fisherman'. He had donated the Tiara for the poor people, and he became the last Pope who wore the Papal Tiara, in history.

Decon Ouseph was lucky enough to be at the Altar of Vatican where the last Coronation ceremony was performed.

The new Pope also liked the black skinned smart young man, Deacon Ouso. He made Ouso as the 'Capo' (Captain) of the Altar Boys of St. Peters Basilica.

The close acquaintance of Ouseph with the old man, Monsignore Michaelosky resulted in developing a strong relationship between them. Ouseph wanted to know more about homeopathy. Michaelosky always talked a lot when it was about homeopathy.

"Homeopathy is a system of alternative medicine created in 1796 by Samual Hahneman. According to him a substance that causes the symptoms of disease in healthy people, would cure similar symptoms in sick people. Making to cure with the cause itself. That is the theory " Michaelosky told Ouseph.

" I think in Allopathy also that theory is being adopted in certain areas."Ouseph said thoughtfully." The snake bites are treated with the venom of the same type of snake which bit the patient. "

"Exactly, you have a good observation power, Ouso, Good, Good." The old man appreciated the Deacon.

"Thank you Monsignore. I am very much interested in your homeopathy. Is there any possibility to study homeopathy?"Ouseph asked.

"Hay Ouso, that is a wise thinking. In my opinion all clergymen should be specialised in one or other professional job, so that, it would be helpful to their fellow laymen. Most of the clergies, mainly diocesan priests are wasting their time and energy by idling themselves. "You should eat with the sweat of your brow," that is what Christ taught. But that is not applicable to diocesan priests."

After saying this Michaelosky laughed. That was a criticism by a priest against priests.

"Will my Rector allow me to study homeopathy as my optional.?" Ouseph doubted.

"Why not. It is permissible. That's how I became a homeo doctor. Priests can be physicians. But not surgeons."

"Why"?

"That is Canon law."

"I am interested to learn homeopathy. How can I learn it?Is it possible?"Ouseph asked with great interest."

"If you want, you can learn homeopathy. It is not that difficult. What required is interest in the subject. There is a Homeo Research Centre about thirty five kilometres away at Gorgeo. It is known as 'OHRC'. Osario Homeo Research Centre. Hundreds of students are studying in that research center."

"Where is it?"

"It is about thirty five kilometer away from here, and five kilometers east to Rocca di Papa."

"Where is Rocca di Papa?"

" I will tell you: It is a beautiful hill station. 'Rocca di Papa" means Rock of Pope. There is a majestic Castle there upon a rock. Pope Eugin third lived in that castle in 1541. Now it is a great tourist attraction. The

Castle is situated by the bank of 'Lake Albino,' yet another tourist spot."

"Lake Albino? What is special about that lake,?" Ouseph was inquisitive to about the place.

"Lake Albino is a volcanic crater lake, situated in the western valley of Alban hills. It is a very huge lake. Its surface area is six square kilometres, and the depth is about one hundred and seventy meters. It is a clean fresh water lake where lot of water games are being organized by the Municipality to attract tourists. "

" Is that homeo school located in Rocca de Papa?"

"Oh, No. OHRC is located in Gorgeo Village, about five kilometres east to Rocca de Papa, in the eastern valley of Albino hills. Though that area, Gorgeo will come under the Municipality of Rocca di Papa, it is considered to be a private province owned by Duke Osario. It is a dukedom. "

" Duke Osario? Still are there dukes in Italy? I was thinking Italy is a Democratic Country."

"Italy is a democratic country, alright. But it allows possession of private property by commune by rendering tribute money to government. The Georgeo's live as a commune, under the leadership of the Duke. The OHRC is owned and managed by the Gorgeo commune. It is a Govt. approved institution and affiliated to Hahneman University west Germany. I was a researcher there about ten years ago."

"You know very well the history and geography of Georgeo Monsignor. It is very interesting."

"We have Capuchin monastery at Rocca di Papa, and I was the Prior of that house for ten years, of course that was about ten years ago. I know both the Gorgeo and the Osario duke families very well. The present Duke is a Catholic Priest; the Parish Priest of Gorgeo Church. Monsignor Baduva Osario, my best friend. He is the only duke priest in our Church. "

"Duke Priest?" Ouseph wondered.

"Yes. Duke priest. By perentage and legacy, Monsignor Baduva is a Duke. For the Church, he is an ordained priest;but he is the ruler of Gorgeo."

"Very interesting."

"Yes. interesting indeed. The history of Gorgeo is linked with the story of Osario duke family. It is very interesting."

CHAPTER 18

OSARIO FAMILY

The history of the Italian village Georgeo was the history of 'Osario Dukedom.' Surprisingly that history had a strong link with Ouseph's life story.

Romano Osario was the Duke of Georgeo. His wife, Duchess Rosabal, was a God fearing noble lady from Venice. They were living in a beautiful white granite castle constructed on the eastern slope of Albano hills. The entire area was volcanic as per the geological map, but never had any erruption for decades; and there were no signs of volcanic symptoms either. The entire region was full of greenery and Georgeo was blessed with its scenic beauty. The last erruption happend in Eighteenth century, and the geological survey affirmed that there won't be any more eruption.

The old duke couple had five children. Baduva, Rancisy, Nicholas, Lissy and Ruth. The two elder children, Baduva and Rancicy were priests, serving in two different churches under Roman diocese.

The third son Nicholas was studying in college at Rome, and staying in college hostel. The two young daughters, Lissy and Ruth ten and twelve years of age were staying with their parents in the Castle, and studying in a convent school at 'Rocca di Papa'

That day, on 8th November 1930, the people at Georgeo village felt a sudden climate change during dusk, which was very unusual. The atmosphere became warm. The western wind stopped. All the perched birds started to fly away. The jackals living in caves and burrows came out of their hideouts and started howling. Pet dogs barked frantically. The Georgeo valley was a deserted place in general. Only vineyards and wheat fields everywhere that belonged to Duke Romano Osario.   The castle was the only lone structure on the slope of the hill. Georgeo village was situated at the far end of the valley on the western bank of Gorgy river. All the villagers, about hundred of them, were the farm workers of the duke.

Suddenly there was a tremendous tremor shaking the entire valley. One of the crests of the hill, where the castle was constructed exploded abruptly with a wild roar, echoing the whole of the region. It was a volcanic erruption, though mild, but its aftereffects were very grave. The beautiful white granite castle collapsed and all inhabitants were smashed to death under the debris. Huge storms and dust along with black molten lava flown out of the crater, that formed on the hill top and it fell over the debris, to bury the castle completely. Later when the molten rocks solidified a gigantic black rock was formed in place of the castle.

That black rock was known to be the 'Castle Rock,' and became a tourist attraction. A heart touching inscription was engraved on the castle rock. It reads " The Osario Duke and his family were buried alive here in the molten lava on 8th November 1930." The names of twenty five people who died in lava also were engraved. The first name was Duke Romano Osario. Then, Duchess Rosa Ball, Lissy, Ruth…and so on…

The elder son of duke, Fr. Baduva Osario, was allowed to take over the assets and affairs of Duke by the curia of Roman diocese, with an intention of taking over the entire property by the diocese on a later stage, after making the younger son Nicholas also a priest. The priests were not allowed to possess any personal assets.

Fr. Baduva Osario was an efficient administrator and a visionary. He divided the total agricultural property of Osario, one thousand and five hundred acres of agricultural land, into one hundred and fifty plots of ten acres each and leased out to one hundred fifty people for Viticulture – cultivation of grapes. He formed a co–operative society of the land lessees, named "Gorgeo Osario Commune" (GOC). It was envisaged to procure the grapes produced by lessees in their vineyards by the GOC. A vinery was established under G.O.C, in the name of "Osario Venery " to produce "Osario Wines" which became very popular in Italy. The members of GOC were allowed to construct their houses in Georgeo village for which they were given free hold lands as plots. They also were given housing loans to construct their houses. A new township was formed. The priest Baduva constructed a good house for Nicholas, in the colony, and   named the house "Osario Villa! ''. He renovated the Georgeo Church and St. Patricia's Church, which was a small Chapal earlier . He established a school and a hospital in Georgeo. He also made a shopping complex under the ownership of the GOC. A committee was formed, for the management of the entire business of Osarios through GOC. Fr. Baduva was the President of GOC.

The greatest contribution of Fr. Baduva was the establishment of OHRC - Osario Homeo Research centre, in affiliation with Hahanan

Homeo University, Germany It later became the biggest Homeo research centre and college in Italy.

Fr. Dr. Michaelosky who was the Prior of 'Capuchin Monastry' at Rocco-de-Papa was appointed as a teacher of OHRC.

Fr. Baduva was known in Italy as "Duke Priest" and he was the Father of Modern Georgeo. He led a humble life of a hermit and led a saintly life.

Rev Fr. Rancisy Osario, the second son of duke Romano Osario, was a newly ordained priest in Sandrio, a remote village at the outskirts of Rome, with lot of beautiful landscapes and wide stretches of meadows. Most of the villagers were farmers and there were many dairy farms. All were conservative Catholics and they were very fanatics too.

Fr. Rancisy Osario was known as a revolutionary. His writings on reformation of Church appeared in periodicals from time to time, which were widly discussed and disturbed the Hierarchy.

An article published by him in 'Messeggero" magazine gave shock to the clergymen, and that became a headache to Vatican. The tittle of the article was "priests and eunuchism."

As per the writings of St. Paul and by canon law, Catholic Priests are to be eunuchs . Fr.Rancisy wrote that those directions are to be reviewed. Anything suppressed by force would be erupted. Sexual urge in human person is very natural and suppressing it by mental control would be sometimes impractical and trying to suppress it by rules and regulations would be considered inhuman, and so it is equivalent to castration by force."

"Allowing catholic priests to marry would no way a effect adversely on their   clerical obligation and church activities, whereas, they would be very free in their mind and would be able to mingle and deal with the laymen irrespective of their gender difference. So it is advisable to allow the priests to marry, otherwise there would be secret breech of adjuration"

His allusions were widely discussed. So many supported his suggestions but were afraid to express openly.

The priest himself fell in love with a Philippino Nun, Sr. Rita Arorya who was a teacher in the church's school. She was a pretty lady with very modest behavior which attracted Fr. Rancisy. He tried to surppress his feelings within him, with prayers and fasting, but of no avail. Day by day the passion increased and he became restless. His close association with the nun had planted a seed of temptation in Rita's mind too. Her heart was eager to accept it. It grew fast and blossomed. Their gestures and close interactions were noticed by many. A scandal was spread out in the village. A Yellow Paper wrote rumours about the priest and nun. Rita was sent out of the convent after a secret enquiry. She was refuged in Fr. Rancisy's Rectory. That night both of them absconded from Sandrio and left Italy. They reached Dubai by a cruise ship. Rita's brother, Jacob Arorya was running a small provision shop with a cold storage near the fruit market in Dubai. The priest of Sandrio, who was son of a duke, became a shop attender!

Fr. Baduva reached Dubai after his brother.

"You should have mentioned about your change of mind. I would have arranged a decent defrocking officially." Fr. Baduva lamented.

He gave him a cheque for two hundred thousand dollars and advised him to develop the business. " If you need more funds, call me" He said.

Rancisy developed the business of a leading milk distribution company in Dubai, in the name of ' Osario Milks. Later the company became a multi crore, international trading business, with change in the name to "Marso International limited'. Its main operations office was in India at Cochin.

The third son of Duke Romano Osario was Nichalos and he was an entirely   different personality.   Nicholas was a naughty, and a jolly good fellow from his childhood. In college, 'communist' youths were his friends. But he was not an atheist. He was a rationalist. A realistic rationalist.

The Father procurator of East Roman Diocese had tried his level best to canvas Nicholas with all his logics and theological arguments, to make him a 'Seminarian'. But Nicholas did not heed to his allurements.

"Your eldest brother Fr. Baduva is a pride of our Church. The other brother is   also equally good and became very popular by his writings. But both are not that proactive types. With your smartness and pro activeness, you would be a bishop in future. Don't you want to follow your brothers.?" Fr. procurator asked .

"I am not a blind follower." Nicholas replied bluntly. The priest got shocked.

"Blind? What the hell you mean? "

"I am talking about their perspective about God. My perspective is different from theirs and yours."

"what is your perspective?"

"God is the inherent power of nature, having no face or figure. God is an Omnipotent Power and a system which controls and governs the entire Universe."

The priest was stunned and he stood agape in front of him."You don't believe in Holy Bible? " He asked.

"Bible is a book of knowledge and wisdom. I don't think it is Holy to be worshipped. It is to be referred and to be followed if you are convinced. I don't blindly believe anything until I am convinced myself."

"Until you learn, you won't be able to convince yourself" The priest argued

"I am not interested to learn in depth and breadth on the presumptions and speculations of some old monks. I don' think the Bible was written by God or given by God "

The procurator got annoyed. He branded him as ' Communist' and left. His idea to enroll him in seminary and attach the entire assets of

'Osarios' to diocese was gone astray. The Diocese imposed a huge amount as a tribute to Osario, and Fr. Baduva had agreed to it. It was a practice in Rome to collect compulsory tributes from the rich and the dukes by the Church, and in return Church protected their interests whatever it might be.

Nicholas was assigned by his eldest brother Baduva to run the 'Osario Vinery' in which different types of "Osario Wines' were produced. The ' Osario Wines' were very popular in Italy.

Nicholas was an efficient 'wine taster'. His profession made him a drunkard. He was in booze all the times. Drunkenness made him a short tempered man. Fishing and cooking were his hobbies. He used to catch fishes from lakes, cook himself and eat and drink along with his friends. In order to save him from the addiction of alcohol, Fr. Baduva removed him from Vinery and made him to run a 'Canteen Cum mess' in the OHRC campus where one hundred staff and students were staying in hostels. Nicholas liked the job. He started to serve, packed fish fry and food to Georgeo's at a good price. "Nicholas Frithura" became very famous . Even from Rocca -de – Papa, people used to come to OHRC to buy " Nicholas Frithura." (Fish Fry)

He married a Georgeo girl, Elenor. They had a comfortable family life. Nicholas – Elenor couples had one girl child, Catherine. When the child was three years old,   Elenor died of a faulty pregnancy. Baduva arranged the girl child to be taken care of by Carmelite Sisters, at Florence . She grew in convent, as a pet of nuns. Nicholas restarted his drinking habit, and died of alcoholism at the age of fifty.

Surprisingly the members of Osario duke family became the main characters in Ouseph's life story.

CHAPTER 19

A CHARMING BLACK

Ouseph was reluctant to approach Fr.Luiz for the permission to go for Homeopathy study. Thrice he went up to the Rector's office and withdrew without meeting him.But that evening, Rector called him to his office and asked, " Ouseph, do you want to go for Homeo studies? "

Ouseph was surprised. He replied with great enthusiasm. "yes father."

"Monsignor Michaelosky told me that you are very eager to study homeopathy. Good. If You could take a B.A degree within four years, by correspondence course it would be a pea nut for you to study Homeopathy."

"Thank you father."

" You may please liaise up with the monsignor and get your admission. Monsignor was a teacher in OHRC Georgeo, long back . That institution is owned by another monsignor, Monsignor Baduva Osario. All call him Duke Monsignor. His father was the Duke of Georgeo."

"But there is a problem father " Ouseph said.

"What is that? "

"Travel would be a problem. There are frequent buses to Rocca di papa. But from there to Georgio there is no line buses. Only private trucks. There is a 'Funiculor' to cross the mountain. But that is meant for tourists and has no regular timing. We have to depend on taxi horse cab. That would be expensive."

Fr. Luiz smiled." Oh….you have already studied about it in detail! Very good. We have already taken care of that problem. You need not depend on public vehicles. We have an old bike kept unused in our store. You can use that motor bike. You can fill the petrol from the Vatican Pump on credit, in seminary's account."

"Oh…that is wonderful. Thank you Jesus. You have taken care of everything "Ouseph's eyes became moistured.

"Before we start thinking, God decides. I am only an agent."

"Yes, You represent Him, Father." Ouseph said very gratefully

Ouseph knew about the unused motor bike that was kept in the store of the seminary. He had learned to ride that bullet bike.   Learning of driving was a part of the faculty of SDA seminary. All the aspirants after passing the 1st phase of the training would learn driving, on all domestically used vehicles.Because the priests from SDA congregation would be posted in mission fields and in war fronts to serve with Red Cross, where the knowledge of driving would be necessary. All aspirants who became 'Deacon's were possessed Italian driving licenses.

Mansignor Michaelosky personally took Ouseph in his Car to OHRC School at Georgeo for admission. They met Monsignor Baduva Osario the Director of the college at his residence attached to St. Patuza church in Georgeo village.   Baduva was young compared to Michaelosky, hardly sixty five. But he was friendly with the old man Michaelosky. They were like buddies.

Ouseph found, Rocca de Papa, the hill station, was very typical and alike to any other Italian town, deserted. Most of the people were using horse cab. Horse riding also was very common.

He had seen the 'funicular' first time. It was one of the modes of transport used in Italian hill stations, which uses a cable traction for movement on steep inclined slopes. Funicular uses two passenger vehicles, forty seats each at a time attached to the same ropes. One vehicle for ascending and the other for descending simultaneously. It passes through Vineyards and eye catching land scapes in the valley of Albano hills.

The general outlook of Georgeo village was entirely different from Rocca di Papa town . It looked like any other modern European township . Identical houses, though small, in lines constructed on both the sides of beautiful roads. He had seen cars parked in front of each house. Georgeo Church beautifully constructed with a high bell tower at the centre of Georgeo Colony..

The OHRC School campus situated two kilometres away from Georgeo colony, in the middle of a wheat field. There were not much of structures in the Campus. A single lengthy house of about four thousand square feet was the OHRC building. There were two separate hostels for men and women, on both sides of OHRC building. There was another single storied building by the entrance of the campus with a board "Mensa" means Canteen. It looked like a hotel. The hostel inmates were dining from Mensa. The Georgeo dwellers used to take packed food from OHRC Mensa.

Ouseph was thrilled to go alone to Georgeo on motor bike. Usually seminarians were not allowed to go out alone. They were to go in pair, or in   group and with written permission from the rector, by "Prenotare," means booking out pass. Ouseph was exempted from all such formalities.

Ouseph felt triumphant, when he dashed out of seminary compound alone, on his bullet bike. His mind was filled with joy and gaiety as of a caged bird let freed. He was having such a feeling for the first time in his life. He wanted to laugh aloud. For him that was a new experience. One would know the thrill of freedom when it was restricted. He wanted to ride faster and faster. He wanted to upsurge to the sky. The traffic was so hectic and he was compelled to reduce the speed that reined his excited mind.

That was a Wednesday, the day of Papal Audience. All the roads in Rome were blocked by traffic jam. To avoid blockades he took a short cut through 'Arabs colony' and reached colosseum.

The colosseum is a gigantic bricks-built stadium like structure, an old monument with an average seating capacity of sixty five thousand people when it was in use during AD 70 – 72,in the Roman Empire. Colosseum was used to stage very cruel entertainments, by making slaves to fight each other with various weapons, until one man fell killed. Slaves were also made to fight with wild animals. The Romans would cheer aloud when the animals tore apart the human body and drag the dead body to their caves that are constructed under the colosseum walls. During the period of suppression of Christianity, Christians were thrown to uncaged lions as their baits of food. The Romans sitting in the gallery would laugh and cheer aloud when frightend small kids and women were chased and killed by the beasts. When the victims cried for help the crowd would mock and enjoy. Those cruel entertainments continued till the end of sixth century. Thousands of Christians were homicided, in the open ground of Colosseum. In 1749, Pope Benedict XIV declared the colosseum as a Holy place and granted "PlenaryIndulgence" to the visitors of Collosseum. Since than it has been a crowded place.

On that day also the area was crowded, when Ouseph reached Colosseum.

He crossed the ring road, reached 'Roma enclave' and turned to right to enter the motor way. The motor way was free of traffic. He accelerated his bullet to one hundred and fifty kilometres and reached Rocca de Papa within ten minutes. He rode through 'Rock Palace road" and by the back of volcanic 'crater lake' and reached the valley of Albano

hills. He passed through the tunnel road and reached in front of 'Castle

Rock.'

The sight of Georgeo village from the hill top, near the castle rock was

beautiful. He could see the Georgeo colony at a far distance, with its

Church tower as its land mark. The entire valley was full of vineyards,

belonged to the Gorgeo commune. He also saw the DHRC complex

situated at a very far distance, isolated.

He rode through the country road and entered the DHRC compound.

He parked motor bike under a chest nut tree and looked around in

bewilderment.

OHRC was providing two types of courses. Research and development

of medicines, and treatment were the main courses: That was a three

years residential faculty. Students had to stay in the campus. There were

two courses for treatment training. Those courses were for the day

scholars. One was in the morning and the classes were from 9am to

12am, and the other one was in the evening from 2 pm to 5 pm.

Ouseph opted for the evening sessions; classes from 2 pm to 5 pm

Ouseph looked at the watch. It was only 1 pm. One more hour was left to start the class. It   took only forty five minutes for him to reach DHRC from Vatican. He was in his Deacon's dress, Cassock.

"Hi, Deacon Ouso, Perche stai Li da solo"?

Ouseph heard a loud female voice in Italian language, meaning "why are you standing there alone ."

He turned and saw an Italian girl standing at the door of canteen and was waving at him.

She asked him loudly again in Italian ."Why are you standing there alone. Please come and be seated in our canteen. Still there is a lot of time left to start your class."

Ouseph was startled. He went inside the canteen very perplexed. The girl sat behind the manager's desk and invited him to sit on a chair opposite to her. He sat and looked around. That big dining hall looked like any other restaurants in Italy. There were two glass panneld almara's behind her desk with full of pastries and bakery items. There were more than twentyfive glass toped tables in two rows and four stainless chairs around each table. The dining hall was empty. He noticed the lunch time "Twelve to one' written on a board.

" Hi, Deacon   Ouso , we are honoured to have a 'Deacon' in our campus." She said smiling.

"How do you know my name?"   He asked

"Who does not know your name in Italy? Your face and name are very familiar to everyone. You were on TV when the Coronation of Pope was telecast. You were the only black skinned man on the Altar. Camera was focused on you several times, when you were holding the Tiara crown, before handing over to Cardinal for Coronation. The commentator said you are Deacon Ouso from India. I thought all Indians are black like you. Later I came to know you are the only black man in India. I like your black colour, this oily black soft skin. You are beautiful in this colour." She gigled loudly

"I am honoured by your compliments madam." He said, and what he said was from his heart.

"Hay, don't call me madam, call me Catherine. you can call me Cathry."

"My mother's name was Kathry. I lost her when I was ten years old. I don't call you by that name."Ouseph said.

"Oh…then call me Catherine. It is a wonderful coincidence. You can consider this Kathry in your mothers place." She laughed again.

Ouseph admired the beauty of that young girl Catherine. She had the colour of a rose petal, soft whitish red. She was about five feet eight inches tall, equal to his own height. She had a blond hair cropped at her shoulder. Her face was beautiful and cheeks were chubby and reddish. Her lips were very rosy without lipstick. She wore a white shirt and black frilled frock that reached up to her ankle.

Ouseph never reviewed a female like that ever before.

"For me it is a shock; some one is telling me my skin is beautiful." Ouseph said.

"Upon God. I am telling the truth. I like your colour, with this smooth skin"

By saying this she placed her both palms over the hands of Ouseph which were kept on the table. Her hands were smooth, warm and delicate. Ouseph felt a sort of pleasant feeling piercing through the skin to his veins, which penetrated up to his brain . Immediately he withdrew his hands as if he was electrocuted.

"Hay, why do you withdraw your hands,You don't like me touching you." Ouseph felt some sort of resentment. .

He thought of St.Paul's words written in the Bible which he had read several times during Mass. "It is well for men not to touch woman. "

On that subject, the Rector taught in the class "By touching a woman, Satan will induce a sensation of temptation in you, which will lead to adultery. Keep away from woman. Never touch a woman.   Let her not touch you."

He got up quickly and ran out of canteen, as if he was frightend.

CHAPTER 20

A WIN TO FAIL

"Rev. Dr. Luiz SDA, Rector, SDA   Seminary Vatican, and the nominated Bishop of Rome, is dead in road accident."

That was the headlines of that day's News Paper The Roman Observer' (L'osservatore Romana)

It was a great shock to Vatican. All who knew him were deeply grieved. Ouseph cried aloud in public, making other seminarians also to cry.

Seven days' mourning prayers were ordered in SDA seminary. There were memorial prayers daily for seven days at the tomb of Fr. Luiz at St. Rita's chapel cemetery at Rome, led by Cardinal Stevensky, bishop of East Rome. Pope himself led prayer one day.

That was one of the major accidents that took place near San Lorenzo chapel, where 'Scala Santa ' was installed.

'Scala Santa' - (English - Holy Stair) was a stair with 24 marble steps   leading to' PRAETORIUM' of the Pontius Pilate in Jerusalem on which Jesus Christ was said to be stepped, on his way to the trial during Passion.

The stair was believed to be brought by St. Helena, the mother of Roman emperor   Constantine,   in A.D 326 and installed in San Loranzo Chapel, which was the private chapel of earlier Popes. Those steps are not accessible to the pilgrim,today. What they do is to stand on their knees and climb the steps on the replica. But, that does not matter to the pilgrims. What they want is to have some stair to step on their knees to enable them to get the 'Indulgence' granted by Pope. Scala Santa is open to the public with an entry fee of 3.50 Euros and Scala Santa would be crowded on all Fridays.

It was on a Friday, the car of Fr. Luiz collided with an over speeding truck, driven by a drunken driver near Scala Santa. Fr. Luiz and the driver died on the spot.

Ouseph brooded and moaned for two weeks. His eyes never dried. His fellow seminarians compelled him to have his food.

Ouseph never did cry when he received a telegram a year back, when his father died in hospital. He did not take any interest to go for his funeral either

Fr. Dr. Andrew Decosty, an Italian priest,took over as Rector of SDA Seminary. He was a well reputed scholar and a strict disciplinarian. He was the principal of SDA college Venice, and later became the Vicar of St. Benedicts Church near Naples.

Being the seniormost priest in the Congregation, he was expecting to become a Bishop. As per his assumption, presumption and self assessment, he was eligible, suitable and very apt to become a bishop long before.. But he was sidelined and bypassed twice by two junior priests which made him upset. Whenever he happened to see the new Bishops with their purple coloured 'Sashes' on their waists and 'skull caps' on their heads, Decosty became irritated and bad tempered. This psychological disorder put him into troubles, even into a serious criminal case, which rocked Rome.

That happened when he was the Vicar of St. Benedicts Church near Naples.

On going through the accounts of the Church he suspected some discrepancies. When questioned the sexton, he replied in a rude manner. That was the time Decosty was in his bad mood. He slaped the sexton on his face in front of the parishioners . He shouted at him and called him a thief.

It was a great insult for the sexton. He was hurt. In fact, he was innocent. The error was in calculation made by the priest himself. That was detected by the auditor, on a later stage.

The very next day of assault , the sexton hanged himself, on a cross beam inside the Church. He had written a death note, in which Decosty was accused of manipulation of accounts.

The local administrative body was governed by Communists. They were anti religious and against priests. They took initiative to get Decosty arrested and it was a big news, in Rome. The entire Italay was shocked. Vatican had to intervene to get Decosty released from the lock up. It became a necessity to transfer him from Naples. Hence he was assigned to take up the Rector post of SDA Seminary.

Fr. Decosty was an optimistic person. "Whatever comes across in life is for good" That was what he believed. The posting at SDA Seminary also was considered to be a blessing in disguise for him. If there was no case against him, he would not have got the transfer to Vatican, which would enable him to have personal contacts with Pope and the Cardinals of Administrative Council. Until and unless one had

' contacts' with higher ups, promotion would not be possible in Catholic Church. That was what he believed.

The new Rector became a nightmare to the aspirants of SDA Seminary. They were afraid of him. Two a spirants who became Deacons left the seminary as they found it difficult to cop up with the new Rector.

The homeopathy study of Deacon Ouso at OHRC Homeo College at Georgeo, near Roca de Papa also was stopped by the new Rector.

"Seminaries' are meant for developing competent priests for the Church, not to make doctors and nurses, was the new Rectors policy. You should have taken some Bible subjects for your optional studies for doctorate." Fr. Decosty said in anger.

Ouseph became very upset. It was not that he had to discontinue the Homeo studies that had upset him, but that he would be missing Catherine, and never would be able to meet her if he discontinued the Homeo studies. Though there were only ten months of friendship with her, a strong intimacy developed between them.

Her friendship with Ouseph started the day when she met him for the first time. She was very well moved by the delicasy and shyness shown by the Indian Deacon.   The sudden withdrawal of his hand from her grip was a shock to her. She decided to brake his shyness and cowardice, when he deals with women, at least with her.

Next   day, when Ouseph was sitting   in   the canteen alone waiting   for the bell to ring for his class, Catherine went to him with a cup of coffee. She placed the cup in front of him and said. "Good afternoon Deacon Ouso. Please try this coffee. It is a special blend imported from Brazil. You will like its flavor. "

Ouseph looked at the girl in wonder. She was smiling charmingly. Ouseph did not smile back.

"I don't want coffee. I have not ordered for one either." He said in an unpleasant tone.

"This is not against an order. It is my compliment. You are my guest now." She pushed the cup further toward to him and sat by his side very close to him.

"I am not your guest. I am a student of this college and I am sitting in the College canteen."   He said with indifference.

She laughed, as he had cut a joke. "Hay deacon Ouso, this canteen is mine. I am the owner. It was started   by my father Nicholas. I am running it on contract basis. Now you are my guest OK?." She laughed again.

" I don't receive any compliments from any unfamiliar person." He said with irritation and pushed aside the cup.

That hurt Catherine, she never expected such a rude behavior from him. Her face fell. Her eyes filled and Ouseph saw her reactions .He felt sorry.

When she was about to take back the Cup, Ouseph caught hold of it, snatched it and sipped the coffee.

"Thank You " He said looking at her face, smilingly.

She also tried to smile. But her eyes were over flowing. Ouseph caught hold of her hand and said."Hay, What is this. Don't be silly. Are you so delicate? By the appearance, I thought you are a tough Italian girl."

Suddenly she put her other hand over his and said. "I am happy Deacon Ouso. Thank you for accepting my coffee."

"Please cut that Deacon part, Catherine, I am just Ouso for you."

"I also don't like that prefix." She laughed

They talked for about forty minutes on that day, till the bell rang for his class. Up to that time he was holding her hand and her both hands were on his.

Their meetings in canteen continued for months and an intimacy with an unknown emotion and affection developed in their hearts. Gradually affection turned to be love and a time reached that it was impossible for both of them not to meet each other even for a day.

Ouso started to miss his classes spending time with her alone at her home "Osario Villa" in Georgeo village. He started thinking of another life with Catherine.   He was thinking how to go out of Seminary. For him it became a foolery to continue in the   Seminary. But he wanted time. Sufficient time to chalk out plans.

It was at that juncture, Fr. Decosty barred him from going for Homeo Study. Some how he wanted to go to Georgio and meet Catherine.

After a lot of thinking, Ouseph gathered himself sufficent courage and went to his Rector to talk.

"Father, tomorrow, I will be assisting Holy Father at his Mass in Sistine Chapel' . He may likely to ask me about my Homeo studies. He always asks. Shall I tell him that you have stopped me from going to Homeo college.?"

Fr.Decosty was taken aback. He stared at Ouseph in wonder and asked.

"Does Holy Father, know that you are going for Homeo Studies.?"

"Why not. Consent letter was signed by our previous Patron Pope himself. His letter would be in the file. It was an order like."

Fr. Decosty suddenly opened the Cabinet, took out the file and perused it. He was shocked.

"Hay Deacon, I was not aware that you were granted permission by Pope himself. You may please continue with your studies. Who am I to stop it, against the order of Pope. Become a good Homeo doctor Priest. Or I would say a Priest Doctor. All the same. Is in't It? May God bless you." He placed his hand on Ousephs's head and blessed with a pleasing smile.

Ouseph had won one game, to get failed in another one.

CHAPTER 21

DEFROCKING

All senior Deacons of SDA Seminary were sent to St. Francis Monastery at Assissi about 180 km away from Rome, for retreat and contemplation. It was a part of training of the aspirants for the psychological shaping of their minds. The course was for one month, and it was mandatory

Usually retreats would give peace of mind and easiness of tension if any. It makes reconciliation with God, and repentance on sins. But Ouseph felt uneasy and became upset. He did not listen to any of the sermons delivered there and was not attentive in the classes. He was thinking of Catherine and Georgeo. His mind was in Georgeo. He wanted to skip all further training and get away. He even thought of running away from the retreat camp. But he did not have the courage.

Catherin's suggestion was echoing in his mind all the time.

"Why don't you get rid of the outfit of the deacon and come out of Seminary and live with me, in my house. I have sufficient wealth for both of us to live together."

Catherine had suggested this, when they were together in a bed in her house, "Osario Villa " at Georgeo.

That was the practice of Catherine and Ouso for the last six months. Whenever she was free in Canteen Ouso would skip his class, go to her house, and spend the whole day with her.

Ouseph was very cautious. He did not jump into action as Catherine had suggested. He knew well of the consequences. The Romans were very conservatives and racists. They were extremists and fanatics too. They won't accept a defrocked deacon in   their commune. They won't hesitate to kill defector of Seminary or Church. Centuries ago, there were a number of martyrs in Rome. Thousands of Roman Christians were brutually murdered and became martyrs during the time of religious oppression.   Now the same Christians turned to be fanatics, racists, and became terminators of defectors from Christianity.

Ouseph tried his level best to talk to Catherin through phone from Assisi. But phone facility was not accessible to seminarians, which made him more upset.

After One month, on completion of the retreat when reached Vatican, he was getting ready   to go to Georgeo. Fr. Decosty the Rector called him and said. "Deacon Ouso. The OHRC is closed for Christmas holidays. They will reopen only on January fifteenth. Now you may please join your brothers to prepare for Christmas. A beautiful crib is to be made. Let us make a good Christmas tree also. Holy Father is likely to visit our Seminary in any of these days. Is in't."?

Ouseph became more upset. His plan to go to Georgeo and meet Catherine became jeopardized.

It was the night before Christmas . Time was about nine thirty. People started to pour in to St. Peter's Square for Christmas celebrations.

 Carol would start at ten. It would last for one hour. At eleven O clock Pope would appear on the open air Altar. A ceremonial Pontifical Mass and a lengthy Christmas message to the world by the Pope would be the main event. As usual, the first reading during the Mass would be the duty of Ouseph. In his absence, the   assistant leader of altar boys would read.

All the altar boys, about twenty of them were changing their costumes in Altar boys room. A Swiss guard came hurriedly into the changing room and announced loudly   "Deacon Ouso, wanted urgently by Rector."

I am on Altar duty." Ouseph replied

"It is urgent". He shouted.

Ouseph left the room in a hurry in his alter costume and ran to Rector's office situated on the eastern block of St. Peter's huge structure.

He was shocked seeing Catherine sitting along with Monsignor Baduva and other two Italians in the parlour of Seminary.

Parlour was a huge hall where meetings of aspirants were conducted.

Fr. Decosty was standing in front of them talking and Catherine was crying. The face expression of Monsignor Baduva was calm , but Decosty's face was red with anger. He could see the flames of fury in his eyes.

Catherine, got up quickly from her seat and walked forward to talk to Ouso. But Decosty blocked her and told to Ouseo."You come with me."

He guided the Deacon to a corner of the parlour away from the guests and told him very seriously. "Look Ouso. You are in deep trouble. Not only you, me, the seminary and the whole of the Church is in a serious problem."

Decosty had difficulty to talk due to over emotion. He was stammering due to rage . Ouseph could not grasp what the Rector was talking about.

"What happened, father?" he asked anxiously.

"That lady, the bitch says she is pregnant, and that was you are responsible. "

Ouspeh was shocked to death. He felt that the entire world was whirling around him. He wanted to sit some where. He leaned on the wall for a support, and looked at his Rector with frightened eyes.

" Don't worry. Don't get upset on this issue. I am not interested to know the truth. I just want you to say that you are not responsible for her pregnancy. That's all. I will help you to come out of this muck. Now only eleven months left for your Pre- ordination course. You are the number one in this batch. Your name has already been forwarded to Papal house for approval. At this juncture, I don't want you to be a dropped out from the list. It would tarnish my name. You just say you don't know anything. I will take care of the rest. If she talks much I know how to silence her." Decosty   was biting his teeth with rage and his faces became reddish.

"We will go to them now. You just say you don't know anything. OK? A small lie. I hope it would save our face and uphold the dignity of our Church.

"No father. If she   said, I am the cause, it must be true. I won't deny it. I won't deny it, though it was an accident." Ouseph said very firmly.

What happened next was very unexpected.

Decosty barked very loudly "You Pig" and he hit Ouseph at his face very violently. His roar was like a wild animal. The entire parlour was shocked by its echo. Ouseph fell on the floor. Decosty raised his booted leg to kick him on his ribs.

"Don't beat me" Ouseph cried.

"Hay , you don't touch him"   Catherine shouted loudly.

Her shrill voice was ear blasting. Decosty was stunned and taken aback frozen. Her sound was a whine of a she lioness. She ran to Ouseph and helped him to get up to his feet. There was a big bruice, on his face below the left eye and blood drops appeared through his nose.

"You have no right to manhandle him" Monsignor Baduva shouted at Decosty.

"I am sorry, Monsignor, I could not control myself."

"That is the trouble with you. You know the consequences?" Baduva asked.

"We will   talk   in my office. Will you please come..." Decosty requested.

Both the priests were alone in the Rector's office. Decosty sat behind his desk and invited Monsignor Baduva to sit opposite to him.

"Decosty, you have all   the right to terminate Ouso from your Seminary. But you have no right to beat him. It is against the Canon law and a criminal offence as per the Italian civil code. If he files a suite against you, you will be in real problem. Already there is a criminal case pending against you in the court. This will add up its seriousness."

Decosty became pale. "Oh. No. He wont have that guts to file a suite against me in Roman court. It is very expensive. He can't afford to meet." Decosty justified.

"But Catherine is an Osario girl and she is rich. She is the heir of the dukedom. Besides she is my only niece."

"Are you supporting him, that barbarian Indian, ? We are Romans. That fellow is a low born   and from a low caste . His father was a grave digger." Hatred reflected in Decosty's eyes.

"Decosty, forget about his past. What he is now is to be considered. That is what Christanity. He is educated and spiritually fit. He is leader of the altar boys of Vatican, and has very close association with Pope. He is very extra ordinary."

"' But, Monsignor, he …" He wanted to say something.

" I know all his stories, Catherine told me everything. I also had a detailed discussion about him with Monsignor Michaelosky. In his opinion, the mistake   might have happened because of my   niece, Catherine, ."

"I strongly recommend you sir please, let her go for an abortion. It is against our Christian ethics, but it will save the diginity of your family and the prestige of my Seminary as well. " Decosty said strongly.

"Then what about him the boy, Ouso".

"I will take care of him. I know what to do. If it wont work out well, I will silence him" He said very casually

Baduva was shocked.

Catherine came running from   the Parlour to rector's room. She pushed open the door violently. Her face was flush with anger. She looked very ferocious. Both the priests got up from their seats in bewilderment.

"What is this daughter?" Baduva asked.

She pointed her finger at Decosty and said "Uncle, he is not a priest. He is a butcher. He told Ouso, that he would silence me if he would deny my pregnancy. I will sue for this for sure."

Decosty's face became pale and of sweat beads appeared on his face.

"Hay I was joking" He said with a stammer.

"But the same thing you told me just now   about him?" Baduva questioned.

"I want to save my seminary and your family from disgrace." Decosty managed to say so, with great difficulty. His throat dried up, and he was shivering.

Baduva stared at Decosty for some time.'

"Monsignor please tell me, what shall I do now.?" He pleaded with folded hands.

"Uncle, I am your only niece. You are more than my father. It is you who brought me up. I am the last child of our lineage. Uncle, I love Ouso. It was me who   started all this. Not him. Now his child is growing in my womb. I love him. And I made him to love me. Of course he loves me and we want to live together. Will you please help us by blessing our marriage.?"

She was crying. Tears rolled down through her cheeks.

Baduva walked towards his niece. He embraced her affectionately and said. " I will dear. I will" .

Then, he turned to Decosty and said "Send Ouso out from Seminary having him dismissed. Settle all his accounts. Pay the full money due to him. Give him back all his documents, Passport and Driving License etc, I will fix something for him."

He said as if it was an order.

CHAPTER 22

FROM ROME TO DUBAI

There was no decoration. No celebration. The marriage of Ouso and Catherine was solemnized at St. Patriza Catholic Church at Georgeo on 29th   December, 1965 without any Pomp and show. The marriage was blessed by Monsignor Baduva Osario, the Vicar, and the president of Georgeo commune. A special sanction was obtained from Bishop of East Rome by Baduva, to bless the marriage   bypassing all routine procedures.

Most of the members of Georgeo commune attended the marriage as it was an obligation for them to attend all functions conducted by the Commune. The marriage of Catherine was considered to be a commune programme.

All the Parishioners who attended the marriage, were bowed in front the bride Catherine and kissed her gloved hand as she was ' Osario duchess': and that was the Roman tradition.

Ouseph the bridegroom in his wedding suite, stood with his bride. Catherine worn white silk gown with a veil and crown, and she looked like a beautiful queen.   Ouseph noticed a visible resentment on everyone's face, when they shook hands with him. Only very few looked at his face, but none smiled or showed any intimacy. Ouseph knew well that the natives were orthodox Romans and they were not in favour of the marriage of Catherine with a black skinned Indian. Over and above, he was a defrocked deacon from a seminary. He was expecting adverse reactions from them. Yet he felt sad when all the natives expressed their discontentment on their faces.

When the couple were escorted out of the Church after the wedding, they saw a placard erected in the Court yard in which it was written in bold letters. "Greeting to the newly married couple. Osario duchess marries a barbarian Indian."

No one knew who erected the placard. There was a contempt on everyone's face. That hurt Ouseph. It was an insult and humiliation in public and he was helpless to react. He could not imbibe the shock and could do nothing about it   He entered the Church, sat on a bench and wept silently. By seeing his desperation Catherin became furious. She stood on a step, clapped her hands to attract the attention of the people gathered and called out loudly.

"Listen all Georgeo's, I am a native of this place and an Osario girl. As the placard says the duchess and also the hair of Osario family. The bridegroom Mr. Ouso is my husband, legally wedded spouse. Now he belongs to Osario family . Any affront on my husband is an insult to me and your Monsignor as well."

It was a caution to Commune members. A threat was hidden in her shrill voice, as most assembled there were very much indebted to Osarios in one way or other.

Immediately the placard was removed. A few gathered around the bride to console her. Many asked pardon for the mischief done by some immature rogue youth.

A grief engulfed in Ouseph's heart. He was disturbed and upset. He wanted to go away from Georgeo to some other place where he was not known to anyone.   He thought of his own native place, Pala.Though lived in poverty and starvation he never lost the self respect.

The love and care showered on him by Catherine did not quench his resentment. He could not recover from his broodiness. He never went out of Osario Villa. He was afraid to face the people.

"Ouso, darling. Please don't get upset.Life is ours. How we live is our own business. It is up to us and do not bother about others. Georgeo is my native place . All those people assembled in the church were the settlers. They all came from other provinces and settled down here as our tenants, and lease holders. Please ignore them. You belong to a duke family now. They are nothing. As long as we are together and our God is with us and only about him that we are to be bothered at all. " Catherine tried to induce confidence in him.

She was going to OHRC every day as usual. The food was bought for them from Canteen from time to time.

Catherine   made a lot of discussion with her uncle Baduva about the future plans. She also talked to her uncle Rancisy in Dubai by phone.

One day Catherine came after her work from OHRC with a telex message from her Uncle Rancisy in Dubai.

"Ouso, darling there is a message for you from our uncle Rancicy . He is inviting both of us to Dubai. Please read it."

She gave him the telex message. It was a very lengthy letter typed on telex printer roll. Ouseph read the message.

"From Rancisy Osario. Osario Milk stores and trades 100, Al Quari Mall Road - Dubai

`Mia Cari figli Catherine & Ouso (Eng : My dear Children)

   The entire letter was typed in Italian Script and it reads :

"My brother ana I Baduva had a detailed discussion over phone yesterday night about you, and we have taken certain decisions to overcome the present crisis in which our family got into. As Catherine is married to Ouso, he is a member of Osario family now.. I could not attend your marriage as it was done very quickly and so did not get sufficient time to arrange my travel. Moreover your aunt Rita is also not doing well. She is suffering from some sort of arthritis though not much serious. The climate here won't suit her well. A change of place is needed for her.

We gladly welcome Ouso to our Osario family. It is God's desire that both of you should join together. God has definite plan for each and everyone in the world, and He has got his   own methods of its implementation. We have to abide by them as it comes. I wish you both a wonderful and happy married life with more children, to take forward the Osario ancestry, as we both brothers have no children.

I understand that Ouso is a bit upset on the ill expressions of resentment made by some miscreants on your wedding day.

Ouso, dear, never get afraid of your own shadow. Romans are conservatives and short tempered curmudgeons in general. But they are not hard hearted as they seem to be . Their enimity would melt away, soon, once you start to interact with them. They won't bother you on your defections from seminary. Now a days defecting even from priesthood is not a big issue to anyone. But that was not the case when I was defrocked from my priesthood.Your aunt Rita and I had to face a lot of harassments and   oppressions   from   fanatic Roman Catholic's. But   later the same people gave both of us a grand reception and honour at the same church where we were serving,when we had sponsored their new orphanage and old age home. Now we are the patrons of those institutions. That is the attitude of people. Time and money will heal everything.

However, as my brother Baduva had suggested, it is better that both of you should move away from Georgeo for sometime.

You can take over my business here so that I can move out from here and settle in Georgeo. Baduva needs a help now. He is getting old and having some ailments too, which he never expresses to others. He found it a little difficult to manage our Vineyards and vinery alone. He has to manage Georgeo commune too. As you know the wealth of Osario's is comoflaged by the commune.

Though Msg.Baduva is very pious and a saintly priest, he is a good entrepreneur and a visionary too. It was a wise foresight of him to form the commune and lease out the land of our dukedom to develop vineyards by others. Otherwise we would have lost the entire property under the land sealing act imposed by Italian Government when the monarchy ended in 1946. Assets of co- operative societies were exempted from the land sealing limit and Georgeo commune is a co-operative society Now it is up to us to maintain what we possess and hand over to our next generation.That is of course through you, and only through you.

My business here is distribution of milk in Dubai. I am importing milk powder from Venice and convert it as bottled milk in blending machines imported from Germany. There are twenty retail outlets in the city for the distribution of 'Osario Milk'. We have fifty agent distributors also. We are blending twenty tons of milk powder everyday to make four hundred thousand glass bottles of milk,five hundred ml each. Though the business is very simple, it involves a lot of work. Importing of milk powder from Venice, bottle from Iran and its packing boxes from Pakistan are complicated, yet it gives very good profit. We have about one hundred employees to work in our blending factory and distribution network and all of them are from India.

I want you to start from Rome immediately on receipt of this letter. On a later stage when I become aged, you may have to manage our Georgio business also. Of course at that time, you will have your kids. You can have your Visas on your arrival. I will be at the airport to receive you, most probably at the immigration counter itself as the Chief Immigration officer Mr. Al Altaff is my friend.

This decision is taken by me and Baduva after a detailed discussion."

Regards., Rancisy Osario."

"Now what do you think?." Catherine asked Ouso," How great is our God. He saw your upsetmind and a quick remedial action is taken"

"I believe in Providence. God brought me from India to Rome.Now He is sending me to Dubai. "

"Yes from Deaconate to Dubai.." Catherine laughed.

CHAPTER 23

COURT ATTACHMENT

Martin became very popular in Cochin. He was known as 'Chandler Martin." But few considered him as a thug, and for some he was a mafia goon, since Hamza Moopan, a known thug was always with him as an aide and body guard. Many knew that he was a smuggler, as he was making a lot of money. But every one knew that Martin was a good man.

Martin was always seen riding on a new Royal enfield' motor bike with Hamza on pillion. Sometimes people saw him driving a Fiat car, with Hamza in the front seat. Martin seldom used the car. The car was mainly used for the transportation of his "Consignments." He had established an office for his business near Mattanchery boat jetty. He also installed two phones, one at his office at Mattancherry and another one at his residence 'Mana', at Fort Cochin.

He helped Maggy, his sister in law, to establish a 'Garments stores' at Fort Cochin, attached to her house, where her father Dicru'z had his tailor shop which was closed ever since he died, two years back.

Maggy had studied embroidery and stenography both as her optional subjects, when she was in high school. Anglo Indian Girls Higher secondary school at Cochin was having European syllabus with job oriented   faculties.

" Maggy liked embroidery more than stenography.   But she got the placement as a stenographer in Govardhan Shipping company immediately after her schooling.

She had enough time after resigning from the job when she became pregnant. After the delivery of the baby also Maggy did not to go for work. She did not like to leave the child, 'Mable' in a "Daycare." It was the practice of mother employees in Cochin to leave their babies under the care of ' Daycare' and go for their works.

"Chechi, why don't you start an Embroidery shop in that old tailor shop of your father? It is lying closed ever since Mr. Dicruz died." Martin asked Maggy one day. "You know the embroidery work very well and it is a trend now adays, that girls use more embroidered garments. Why don't you make use of that shop?"

"Oh, that space is not sufficient Martin. It is already very conjusted with one tailoring machine and a cutting table. I need at least two more machines and one more big table to start the embroidery work. It has to go along with stitching There is no sufficient space for all those things."

"Why can't we extend the building further twenty feet towards the road side? If we remove the garden and cut down the bushes, there is ample space in front. Better to do some interior decoration and glass paneling to give the look of a modern shop." Martin suggested.

"Oh…No…that cost a lot of money.",

"Don't bother about money. I will take care of that."

That day itself, Hamza brought a civil contractor from Jew Town He was an interior decorator too. Within four months of continuous work by ten labourers, a beautiful spacious show room was completed. A plastic sign board was erected in front of the shop   "Maggy's Garments Stores!"

Martin brought two automatic Japanees embroidery machines and a stitching machine, which were smuggled out of a Korian ship and that made the shop highly sophisticated and modern.

To purchase of Bombay-made plain garments from Ernakulam Cloth Bazar at a cheaper rate, get them embroided in the machines and sell it   at a higher price was the business.   It became highly profitable, and Maggy's Garments became very popular in Cochin.

Michael was compelled to   resign from Gorvarrdhan   Shipping Company to help Maggy in her business and to take care of the child and house.

One   day Maggy told   Martin. "Marty, brother, please don't get offended if Chechi openly tells something."

"Why   Chechy, Why do you want a prefix in advance to tell me something. You have all the right to tell me anything." Martin smiled.

"Marty, without your money we could never have achieved this shop and the progress. But I am deadly worried about the source of your money. My humble request and prayer is that you please stop your smuggling business. It is very dangerous. If caught, everything would be ruined. Your chettan is not at all efficient to face the situation if anything happens like that." She said very seriously, and   looked worried.

"Chechy,you are right. I am also thinking of stopping my Chandller business. I   want to become an exporter and am looking for an opportunity for that. Don't worry…" He pacified her

" That's good. And another thing Marty. That is also very important. Why don't you marry that girl Sobha and live peacefully together. Suppose something happened to her it would be very serious. You don't spoil her life. She is a nice girl..."

Martin's face fell. Yet he smiled and said. "Chechi, I am not that stupid to spoil a girl."

"Then why don't you marry her?. All know how both of you live. Why, delay? won't she be baptized and become a Christian? . Even if not, don't bother . You marry her in the Register office. We all will support you."

" It is not that. We have not talked about it yet. Anyway I will think about it." He said thoughtfully and left.

In those days Cochin Port also was a hub of smugglers like any other Port in India. Customs and   Security arrangements were not that effective till 1970. Large quantity of smuggled goods were trafficked through Cochin Port. Gold, house hold articles, electronic items radio parts and watches were the main items smuggled out of Cochin wharf. Martin was a very small timer compared to other big smugglers. His commodity was only liquor bottles. Country arrack   bottles were for on board sale and foreign liquor bottles were taken out of ships for local sale, and he was doing it very well.

He was utilising the upstairs of his rented house   'Mana' as his godown, where goods, foreign liquor and country arrack, were stored in bulk. He made Sobha, as his store keeper and accountant. In return he was paying one thousand rupees per month to Bhageerathy Amma, which made her silent, as Martin was the only resource of her income.

Martin was meeting the entire expenditure of the family, including the educational expenditure of Prabha, the younger one of Sobha.

Prabha also was equally beautiful as Sobha, and they both looked alike. Prabha was very studious. She obtained highest marks in SSLC and Pre degree examinations. She was a very good dancer like Sobha. She won the 'Kala Thilakam ' medal in Inter College Youth Festival. All those merits were considered and made her eligible for   Medical college admission in a campus selection, conducted by the Medical Board.

Prabha was well aware of the huge expenditure involved in Medical studies. But she was confident that it would be met by her "Annan" - colloquial addressing   for brother in laws. She was addressing Martin as " Annan" and she was very sure her Annan would marry her

'Chechi' Sobha and he would never deceive her. She had ignored all the ugly scandals spread among the college friends about her 'Chechi' and 'Annan'.

Martin did not have any difficulty in marketing his 'Consignments'. Hamza was his distributor, and the customers were Bar attached Hotels, in and around Cochin city. Even from nearby towns, Bar owners used to come to Cochin in search of Martin for foreign liquor bottles. His trading was against advance payments . Fifteen percentage of the profit was disbursed to Customs and Port officials, as a routine ' Bakshees! for the smooth operation of his business.

Yet he knew that it was   a risky business and an indecent profession. He wanted to get rid of it on getting an opportunity to start an export business.

That day, it was about eight o clock in the morning . Martin was getting ready to go to his office, when he heard a cry, from the court yard.

"Oh…. My God, Marty…. Marty…. Please come…."

The cry was from Bhageerathy Amma. Martin opened the door and ran down the steps. He saw Bhageerathy Amma lying on the floor in the court yard, under the stair. Sobha and Prabha also came running to the spot, where, Bhageerathy Amma was lying. When the girls were crying aloud, Martin brought his car and stopped at the gate.

Martin had purchased the car a few months back for his business purpose. Transporting of liquor bottles; smaller quantity, would be safer in a car.

He lifted Bageerathy Amma in his arms and made her lay down on the back seat of the car. Sobha also sat in the back seat and placed the mother's head on her lap. Prabha sat in the front seat. Marin drove fast the car to Fort Cochin hospital.

"I feel much better now. I think I can sit. " Bagerathy Amma said, though feebly. She tried to get up to sit.

" No Amma. You lie down." Sobha said, by forcing her mother to lay down.

"Marty, I was coming to meet you, my son. I wanted to show you a letter, I received yesterday. While climbing the steps, suddenly I felt a giddiness and became blind. I did not know the fall. " She said.

"What letter she wanted to show me.?" Martin asked Prabha, who was sitting in the front seat.

"I don't know Anna." She said helplessly.

"What letter Amma? You never told me about it.?" Sobha also was unaware about the letter.

Bhageerathy Amma drew out a folded paper which was kept safely inside her blouse and gave to Sobha.

"What is that Sobha?" Martin asked.

Sobha unfolded the paper and read it. Her face became pale. It was an attachment order form the Munsiff Court.

CHAPTER 24

POWER OF ATTORNEY

Bhageerathy Amma felt better when they reached hospital. She was prepared to walk from the car to 'Causality ward', though a stretcher trolley was brought by an attender. " I don't want to lie down on the stretcher. I prefer to walk" Bhageerathy Amma said.

"You look very weak and tired. Better not to walk."

When Martin insisted she lay down on the stretcher. The attender pushed the trolley. The duty doctor was not present and they were made to wait outside the causality. Martin, Sobha and Prabha, sat on a bench. Martin read the letter again and asked Bhageerathy Amma, who was laying on the stretcher trolley.

"What is this Court attachment Ammai.? Our house Mana is ordered to be attached ex-party against a petition filed by one Khassim Sait. What is this?" Martin asked.

Bhageerathy Amma looked at Martin very pathetically. Her eyes were over flowing. Martin understood that there was something very serious behind it.

"Do you know anything about it?" Martin asked Sobha.

" I know Khassim Sait. I was thinking that he was one of the clients of our Achan (father). But never knew Achan had financial dealings with him." Sobha told.

Then, Bhageerathy Amma explained the case in a very weak tone.

Khassim Sait was a pawn broker, who was giving secured loans to people against personal property as collateral security. His interest rate was exorbitant. Customers need to pay a fixed amount per month as interest against the loan.   It would come about sixty percentage per year. Twenty   years ago, Sankara Narayanan had availed a loan of one hundred rupees from him for the purchase of the house 'Mana' from a 'Kongini'. He was paying the interest without a break till four years back, and was compelled to be in arrears due to his ailment. Khassim Sait filed a case for the attachment of house, for twenty five thousand rupees inclusive of interest and compound interest. The interest paid till four years back was not considered as no receipts were produced along with counter petition, filed by Sankara Narayanan, nor did he appear in the court for hearing. As such the verdict was exparty.

Martin understood the case was very complicated. "We have to consult an advocate. It seems, we are in trouble." He said.

"Will we lose our house son? Will my daughters become homeless my son?" Bhageerathy amma asked with   frightened voice.

"No ammai, I am here to take care of everything." Martin consoled by patting her hand.

" I know my son. You are my son though not born in my womb." Her eyes over flowed.

Bhageerathy Amma was taken to examination room and Martin and the two girls waited outside. Their waiting was very long.   After an hour, they   were called in.

Doctor Varrier, looked curiously   at Martin and the two girls sat in front of him

"Are you the children of the patient lady?." He asked.

" I am Martin, her tenant, These two girls are her daughters. " Martin said.

" He is like her son, Doctor. No he is her son.! Sobha said.

"He is our brother" Prabha added." Elder brother. My Annan". Her statement was confirmative and a declaration.

"Yes…Yes… I understood. How is your financial situation?" Doctor enquired

"Why that question Doctor? " Martin asked.

"Because, I am afraid, the treatment would be a bit expensive. How long   was she under ailment? She   told me that she was taking Ayurvedic medicines for a long period.''

"Amma, and my Achan were very addicted to Ayurveda Medicines." Sobha said.

"Ayurveda is good for some type of external ailments, but would have adverse effect on certain internal problems."

"What is the problem with Amma? Is it serious"?

"Please don't get upset when I tell you the truth. She is attacked with cancer. Abdominal Cancer, and it is in its secondary stage. Any way , you have to know it."

 All were shocked. Prabha burst out crying. Sobha was trying to control herself from crying. Yet her eyes filled and tears were flowing uncontrollably. She bit her lips and griped Martin's hand very tightly.

"Will she survive.?" Martin asked.   His throat chocked.

"That is up to God. I will try my level best to save her. But an operation would be mandatory and it would be a bit expensive."

"How much does it cost?"

"About four thousand rupees."

"That is OK with us doctor. Please do the needful."

"But no guarantee. That is up to God."

"I understand doctor."

"Then get her admitted."

"OK."

Bhageerathy amma was admitted in the hospital in 'Pay Ward." She was not told what her ailment was. Instead she was it was only a small tumour, and need to be removed. Operation was scheduled for the fifth day after completion of all the tests.

Martin met Advocate Ramanujan in his office and discussed the attachment order received from the court. After studying the paper the advocate said." Poor Sankara Narayanan Sir, He was my Senior, alright. But he never was a good advocate. He was cheated by everyone in this world. He being, an advocate, could have easily got out of the trap of that Khassim sait., That Sait is a rascal."

" Now, what to do sir, that is my problem."

 Martin revealed him the current situation of the family. He also told him that he was planning to marry Sobha.

"Any way, the money has to be paid as the Court Order was already issued. Now the only way is to go for an appeal in higher Court. But we have to deposit at least sixty percentage of the claimed amount in the court to get the appeal accepted. Even though, no surety of getting the payment waived, Maximum what we get would be a defferment. That we can get even without an appeal. We will ask for the payment on installment basis. We ask for ten installments of two thousand and five hundred rupees per month."

"Can you request for one thousand rupees per month."

" I don't think court will accept."

"Ok. Then proceed. " Martin agreed.

"My fees will be thousand Rupees. That also to be paid in ten installments."

"Accepted."

"Look, Martin. What benefit will you get by spending this much of money for that women?." Advocate asked.

"I told you I am planning to marry the elder girl."

"So? What about the mother and the younger one.? They also have the

equal right of the property. Twenty five thousand rupees is a very big

amount. A building could be purchased by that. When you pay that

much for them you should get the right of the property. Otherwise one

day they will defy and deceive you . Don't trust women. "

Martin thought for a while.

"What should I do sir?" He asked.

"We will make them to sign a power of attorney on your name,

allowing you to deal with the property even to sign a sale deed on

behalf of late Sankara Narayan. I will get it registered and that would

turn to be a deed on your name, and you would have the absolute right

on the property."

"But. is it is necessary?" Martin   said doubtfully.

"Absolutely necessary. Otherwise you would became a fool   one

day."

"Then it's ok" Martin agreed.

That day evening, Advocate Ramanujan went to hospital along with

Martin to meet Bhageerathy Amma and her daughters. He explained to them that they have to sign the power of attorney in the name of Martin to enable him to appear before the Court on behalf of them. They agreed and signed on the stamp paper, which he had brought along with him.

" By this document the house would be owned by Martin after the paying off the debt. Hope you won't have any objection." Advocate told him.

"What objection Sir, I am happy and thankful to him for all these favours he is extending to us." Bhageerathy Amma said   gratefully.

Bhageerathy had to be rushed to the operation theater on the second day as she had vomitted blood.

While preparing her for an urgent surgery she breathed her last lying on the operation table, in the presence of the surgeon and nurses. The anesthesia given to her caused   a heart attack.

CHAPTER 25

THUG TACTICS

The dusk was fast approaching. West horizon was seen painted pink. The sun became a fire ball before desending into the ocean and the sea became reddish. The atmosphere had a sad look.

There was no big of crowd at Cochin Municipal Crematorium, located at the seashore, when the body of BhageerathyAmma was cremated. Michael and Maggy along with their two year old child Mable, were present throughout the funeral. Hamza and his assistants, five agile Muslim youngmen were very active throughout until the body was brought from hospital to crematorium. They acted even as the pall bearers as there were no relatives to help Martin to carry the dead body from the vehicle to the crematorium trolley. A few neighbors of 'Mana', most of them shop keepers, also were present.

When the cremation was about to finishover, a taxi car came to the graveyard and stopped at the entrance. Three people came out of the car in a hurry. One was an aged tall man of about sixty years of age wearing long cloth and Juba Shirt. The other one was a fatty woman in silk saree and wearing of gold ornaments. The third person was a handsome lofty youth with trimmed beard.

The aged person walked directly to Martin who was standing a little away from the crematorium and talking to his brother Michael and Hamza. The ladies, Sobha, Prabha, Maggy and three neighboring women were sitting under a banyan tree very close to the crematorium. All were waiting for the cremation to finish.

"Who is Martin?"

The aged man walked directly to Martin and asked.   His body language and the way of his asking was very authorititative, which was not liked by Martin.

"It is me..who are you?" Martin asked.

" I am a Maman of Sobha and Prabha." He said proudly.

"Maman? What do you mean?"

"Oh… you are a Christian. I forgot that. We Hindus have a different way of addressing our relatives. Maman means Uncle." The aged man explained and laughed.

"Here in Fort Cochin, Mama means pimp". Hamza said, with a contempt.

The aged man's face fell. He looked at Hamza angrily.

"Hay Mr.Maman, don't bother about his comment. If you had told that Maman was a colloquial word for uncle, he would not have reacted like that. But you were glorifying your cast. That was unwarranted . If you are the Maman of the girls why were you asking for me?" Martin asked.

" I heard a lot about you that you are pretending to be the guardian of the girls."

" Yes, indeed. What you heard was correct. I am their guardian.   What do you want actually? If you want to meet the girls, they are sitting right under that banyan tree along with other women"   Martin pointed his finger at them.

Sobha and Prabha came to them. Martin noted   the young man with beard greeting Prabha by a gesture. But Prabha did not respond to it and she was expressionless.

"Sobha, do you know these people?" Martin asked. " He says he is your Maman or something like that."

The aged man responded quickly. "It is my mistake. I should have introduced myself properly. I am Kesavan Unni , from Edacochin, cousin of late Sankara Narayanan, the father of these girls,   rather his mothers sister's son. His aunt's son. We live in Edacochin." Then he continued, at the womon " This is my wife Ammini, and this is my son Sabu. He studied in Maharaja's college. Prabha knows him. "

"Do you know them?" Martin asked Sobha again.

" I have never seen them. But I heard Achan was telling about his aunt at Edacochin?" She said.

"Yes..that is it. That aunt is my Mother. " Kesavan Unni laughed.

"But, these girls don't know you.?"

"Yes. Yes. That is my   mistake. Our mistake. I should have taken initiative to patch up and maintain the relations. It was broken due to nobody's fault. It was the destiny. What else to say about it. Anyway, still there is a lot of time. No,this is the time. The very apt time indeed. When their father and mother had gone, they should not feel that they are alone. We relatives are here to take care of them. Their aunt, my wife Ammini is very eager to take them to our home at Edacochin. Our suggestion is that the girls would stay with their aunt at Edacochin, not alone at Mana !!" Kesavan Unni was trying to establish relation.

" I don't think they need any support now" Martin said firmly.

"Who are you to tell that?" The young man Sabu, with beard intervened suddenly.

"You are a Christian, another caste . We are relatives and Hindus. We have some moral obligation towards our own blood." Kesavan Unni argued.

"I think these fellows are nettle mites.'' Hamza said to Martin in a lower voice. But all heard what he had said in his rough tone.

"Who the hell are you?" Sabu raised his voice.

Hamza steped forward and told Sabu, looking sternly at his face. " I am Hamza. People call me Hamza Moopan. Do you want to know more about me? "

Hamza Moopan. !! The notorious criminal and wrestler of Cochin.!

Sabu had heard a lot about Hamza Moopen. Father of his friend Kumaran, a Trade Union leader has been bed ridden for the last four years after an encounter with Hamza Moopen!

"Hamza is a ruthless devil." That was what Kumaran had said about his opponent Hamza. Now that devil is right in front of him! Sabu got frightened.

"Achan. Let us leave now. We will go to the girls house another day for a talk."

Sabu pushed his father out of the graveyard. His mother followed them.

"They have come here not to pay homage to your mother. They came to establish a relationship and they have something in their mind." Martin told the girls.

That night, after the dinner, Martin, Sobha and Prabha were sitting in the drawing room of Mana reviewing that day's events at crematorium.

"What was the motive behind the visit of that Kesavan Unni and his family at the funeral. Have you ever seen them?" Martin asked Sobha.

"I think I saw that Maman when I was a child. When and where I don't remember now. "

"I know Sabu. What they said was correct. They are our relatives." Prabha said. Her voice was doubtless and there was a discomfiture on her face. Martin and Sobha looked each other.

"Why? What happened?   You look very uncomfortable?" Martin asked.

"I told only Sabu to come there"

"When?."Sobha asked in wonder.

"I telephoned him from hospital's public booth."

"How do you know Sabu?" Martin asked.

"Sabu was my senior in college" There was a flush in Prabha's face.

"You were in college only for two years.?"

" That much time is more than enough to know a person - is it not?"

 Martin did not like the way she talked.

"What is he to you? Any particular interest?" He asked.

"Don't interfere in my personal affairs." Her reply was very sharp and that was very unexpected from her. Both Martin and Sobha were shocked.

What happened next was also very unexpected and shocking. Sobha slapped Prabha at her face very hard. And she shouted to her sister."What an ungrateful creature you are. Stupid. Is it the way you talk to your Annan,   with whom we are living now. Apologise him. Apologise." She shouted.

Prabha never expected such an action from her Chechi. She was astounded and shocked. She covered her face with both hands and cried loudly. That was the first time Sobha was beating her sister in the whole of her life.

Prabha ran to the bedroom, fell on bed and cried aloud.

"You should not have beaten her like that. It was too hard." Martin sympathized.

"I will kill her, if she talks again like that."Sobha shouted for Prabha to hear.

She turned to Martin with tearfull eyes. She folded her hands and told him "I beg your pardon for her ungrateful talk. Please forgive us Martin." Then she wept.

Martin held her shoulders with both hands and he looked at her innocent face for a long time. He had seen a deep love in her. He embraced her very tightly, as she was everything for him in the world.

****

It was about Eleven O clock before noon. Sobha was busy in kitchen preparing lunch. That day Prabha did not take her lunch box as she went to college to collect her certificates. She was asked to join Medical college by the weekend.

Martin started taking his lunch from home, Mana, after the establishment of his office at Mattanchery near boat jetty. There was only ten minutes drive by bike from office to Mana. It would take fifteen minutes by ear as traffic at Palace road would be very heavy.

Unexpectedly someone rang the calling bell. Wondering who that would be, Sobha went and opened the front door. She was shocked to see the 'Maman, Kesavan Unni from EdaCochin standing at the door with a wide smile. She also saw two tough looking ruffians having identical stout figures standing behind him.

"'Maman has come all the way from Edacochi to talk to you personally on a very important matter Sobha, daughter. Hope that Christian lad is not inside. I know he would be away at this time."

"You mean Martin?" Sobha asked.

"Yes… Yes… That is his name…isn't it?"

"He is in the office. Will come by one o'clock for lunch."

"Oh..you cook for that Christian also."

"What do you want Mama? I am busy in kitchen right now" Sobha said with irritation.

" I told you, I have come to tell you something very important."

"Then tell me. I told you I am busy? "

"I will sit and talk." He entered the house.

The two ruffians were also about to follow him. Sobha blocked them and said "Let these two gentlemen be outside. I am alone in this house…" She objected

"Yes…Yes.. That is correct. Hay, you two, be outside. I will call you when I need you." Kesavan Unni told them.

"What do you want them to do inside my house?" Sobha asked.

Kesavan Unni entered the drawing room and sat on a chair authoratitively.

"Daughter Sobha, I am your Maman from same blood and same family. I have some responsibility on you.." He said.

"What do you want? Talk and finish it off." Sobha said angrily.

"It is not at all good, that you are allowing that Christian unmarried youth to live in this house where you two young unmarried Nair girls are living. There were serious discussions on this subject at our Nair's' forum and we decided to compel you to evacuate that Christian man from this house. It he won't agree to leave the house, we will throw him out by force. That's why I brought that two persons along with me. They are our bill collectors of our Society's chit fund. They will be tough if any one acts tough with them. They were in jail for some murder cases."There was a threat in his voice.

"Why do you want him to be vacated from my house. He is a very nice person. He is very helpful to us. At presently we live on him. "

"Sobha, daughter, you don't know the feelings of our Nair Community. We are all Hindus. He is a Christian and our group is against his living with you. It is against our religious ethics. Secondly, our society is planning to establish a branch of our Chitty Company at Cochin, and this house is very apt for a business establishment. Sabu is the manager of the chitty company. Sabu has some other plans also in his mind with this house. After all he is going to be your brother in law. He likes Prabha, and my family has no objection for their marriage..." Having said this at a stretch, he laughed with self contentment.

"Mama, will you please sit here for some time. You can read the newspaper lying on the table. Meantime I will get you a cup of tea." Sobha pretended to be hospitable and hurriedly went out of the drawing room.

"That is a nice thinking Sobha daughter, I am a diabetic patient. Need to put only less sugar." Kesavan Unni called out.

Sobha went to her bed room and telephoned Martin. When he picked up the phone, she said in a frantic voice."Marty. please come quick . We have a miscreant entered into our house. Hurry… Hurry.."

Martin heard the sound of her panting.

"Hay, calm down Sobha. who is that person? What does he want."? Martin asked

She explained in brief about the visitors and told what the Maman had told her and hung the phone.

Martin rode his motor bike with Hamza behind him at a lightning speed and reached 'Mana' within four minutes.

Hamza saw the two ruffians standing at the gate of Mana like watchmen. He recognized them. One was Kannan and the other was Karunan. Both were unloading workers of EdaCochin labour Union, and their leader was Kumaran, who had an encounter with Hamza three years ago at Warf. Hamza had to award Kumaran Scortun hit. And Kumaran was bed ridden thereafter and yet unable to walk.

Both Kannan and Karunan became perplexed when they saw Hamza Moopan right in front of them as if he had appeared from no where. Both of them knew him well and they were frightened to death.

"Why are here?" Hamza growled at them.

"Hamza Bhai. Please don't beat us. We never knew you are involved in this case. " They pleaded helplessly.,

" I am involved in all the cases of Cochin. If you don't want to taste my Scortun hit, as your comrade Kumaran had tasted. Please fuckoff from here now. And do not show your anus again in Cochin."

Both of the ruffians went away, immediately without a word.

The sudden appearance of Martin, and Hamza jolted Kesavan Unni. He jumped to his feet and shivered like a frightened kitten.

" DoYou have phone here? '' Kesavan Unni asked with a surprised tone.

"Why ? Do you want to make a call?", Martin asked, "Sobha told me everything that you had told her." You don't allow them to live peacefully"?

"Please don't hit me. I am a heart patient." He pleaded.

"I wont hit you now. But if you step in this house again, I will, for sure. Now listen. This house is in my name. I paid money and purchased it from the court as it was under litigation. And one more thing. I am going to marry Sobha by next week. Understand? Hope you know everything and it is clear to you. Now you may get out.and never come here again."

" I will never come…"

The old man went out of the house hurriedly.

CHAPTER 26

MANA TURNED TO MANSION

It was quarter past twelve when Prabha alighted from bus at 'Amman coil' bus stop, about one hundred meters away from 'Mana', her house. She was coming from Ernakulam, after collecting her certificates from college. She saw Kesavan Unni standing at bus stop waiting for his bus to Edacochin. He appeared to be desperate and tired. His shirt was drenched in sweat. Prabha felt pity on the old man. She greeted him with respect.

"Hi Maman, why are you here? Haven't you gone to my house?" She asked.

"Yes…Yes… I went to your house to discuss about your marriage. I thought to get it confirmed, with your sister Sobha. But that Christian fellow staying in your house as your guardian threw me out of the house. Sobha was in his side to assault me. It was disgracefull, I am humiliated and hurt."

The old man said in sorrow. He was at the verge of weeping.

Prabha was shocked. She never expected such a cruel act from her sister, towards Maman when he had approached her with the marriage proposal for her.

"Is she jealous on me for getting married with a handsome young man, when she stays still unmarried? Prabha doubted.

Prabha was a typical silly girl, without any discernment, be as she was the younger of the house who received a lot of indulgence from every one. She was always led by emotions. She had the habit of jumping into conclusion on every thing before studying the subject and later regret about it.

"I am so sorry Maman. I don't know why they treated you like that. Surely I will ask them. Forgive us." She said with an apologizing gesture

" That's OK my dear girl. You are a nice girl. That's why Sabu like you. I also like you! But your sister Sobha is a vicious woman. She has already spoiled herself by that Christian ruthless fellow, Martin. I can make out from her body language that she had been seduced by that beast. Let that not happen to you. Don't allow him to touch your body. You are my son Sabu's girl. And one more thing. As long as that

Christian fellow is living in that house, I don't think your marriage with my son Sabu would ever be possible. Our Hindu community will never agree…."

As the bus arrived, the old man got into the bus hurriedly without biding farewell to Prabha. She became upset.

She started walking towards Mana, her house. She was in deep thoughts and mentally disturbed. She knew that there were certain facts hidden in Mamans accusation. It was a fact that Chechi and Annan were living together like husband and wife. Why don't Annan marry Chechi? As long as Annan stays in Mana, her dream of marrying Sabu would never be materialized . That's what Maman had said.

She had seen Martins car coming out of the gate of Mana, with Hamza at its driving seat. She knew Hamza was on his way to deliver liquor bottles to various hotels in the city. She was also aware, that the upstair portion of the house, where Martin was living earlier was changed as liquor store.

If a Police raid takes place, Martin would be booked and end up in jail. Suddenly a devilish thought entered into her mind. An anonymous letter to the Police would solve her problem. Annan would be removed from Mana by Police.

Suddenly she thought back with a jolt. If Annan got arrested, her Chechi also would be taken into custody along with him, as she was involved, as a part of 'Annan's operations. Most of the time Chechi was doing the delivery of 'consignments' by car. The car was purchased and Chechi was taught driving only for that purpose. A woman driven car would never be subjected to a thorough check by the Police.

Prabha regretted herself for having thought of such an ungrateful devilish act of treachery.

She reached home, in utter confusion and desperation. She found Martin sitting in the drawing room on a sofa, and Sobha was by his side very close to him. They were discussing some subject very seriously.

" You may be hungry. Food is served and kept on dining table. Have your lunch" Sobha told her with a mother's affection.

"I suggest both of you get married as early as possible. In my opinion Annan become a Hindu and join our community." Prabha said with a swollen face and arrogant expression.

"What are you talking Prabha?" Sobha was surprised, by the way her sister had talked. The change in her attitude did upset her.

"People are   talking a lot of things about both of you. It is a wonder that you two are not at all bothered about it. I feel ashamed. I want Annan to join in our community and the marriage would be conducted in a temple.?"

" From where do you get the community feeling now? " Sobha asked angrily. When did you start thinking about the community? When our Achan and Amma died where were was community? When our house was, under litigation, where was your community? Now this Saturday we have to remit three thousand rupees for your Medical College admission, and every month you may need more than seven hundred to eight hundred rupees for your hostel fees. Will your so called community remit that amount for you?" Sobha was very furious and her voice was high pitched.

Prabha became perplexed. She just stood in front of them unable to talk. She never thought of such things. Never had any thinking on reality. Sobha's harsh words opened her eyes. She started weeping.

"Prabha, please come here." Martin called her.

When she went near him, obediently, crying, he held her both hands and made her to sit near him. He put his hands over her shoulders and made her to be very close to him. He caressed on her head with lot of affection.

"Prabha, have you seen that old man while you were coming home? " He asked.

His guess was correct. " Yes, I saw him at the bus stand, and we talked." She said.

"What did he talk.?"

"He told me that he came here to fix up the   alliance between me and Sabu. But you and Chechi together assaulted him and threw him out of the house."Prabha said.

"Now I feel I would have kicked that old idiot. He   is a bastard." Martin said

"Prabha, he   had not come here with alliance proposal. He wanted us to send away Martin from this house and give him the up stair portion of our house for his son to do some business. He had brought two thugs along with him to throw Martin out by force. Hamza made them to flee. When he came to know that the house is already in the name of Martin, procured from the court by remitting the litigation amount, he became baffled. He had tried to induce the community feeling in me also as he did to you'' . Sobha said .

"Do you like that man Sabu." Martin asked.

"Yes." Prabha said strongly.

"Are you in love with him?"

"Yes."

" For how long?."

"From college, for the last few months."

"Does that boy love you?."

"Yes."

"We will think about your marriage after you complete your medical studies. First you take your MBBS degree. We will get you married with that fellow, provided he has some earnings to feed a family.

Presently he has got nothing, that I can make out from his look. He is still leaving on his parents. Till you complete your studies please keep away from him. That old man, so called your Maman is poisonous and very vicious. You promise me that you will not   contact that fellow Sabu and his father Kesavan Unni until you complete your studies."

Martin said and he has shown his palm extended to be promised by her. Prabha placed her hand over Martin's and said " promise."

"OK. Then it is settled. Now be a good girl and go and have your lunch." He said.

Prabha could not keep up her promise, and that put her in to troubles   In to very deep troubles.

Prabha joined Alleppy Medical College next Monday. Martin and Sobha went along with her for her admission.

"Whenever, you are in need of anything, please don't hesitate to give me a call. I will reach here within two hours. OK?" Martin assured her.

On that day onwards Martin and Sobha were alone in that house 'Mana." And the Mana turned to be their Mansion.

CHAPTER 27

START OF AN INDUSTRY

There was a great change in Martin's life. That was due to the personal influence of Maggy, his sister in law. She involved and interfered in his life very authoritatively.

She forced him to stop the Chadler business and its allied trading.

She encouraged him to "Shrimp and Prawns business."

Shrimps and Prawns are important Sea food, widly available in Cochin.

"Shrimp is a stinking stuff:" Martin commented.

" Smuggling is poisonous and killing." Maggy retorted.

Procure raw fresh shrimps from the fishing boats, get it peeled and de – wained in peeling sheds, then freeze it in freezing plant, pack them in cartons and export was the business, Maggy had proposed.

"Though the work involved is tedious, it is a lucrative business." Maggy said.

There were separate contractors to undertake each of the processing works from peeling to packing, and that wasnot a big deal.

The toughest part of any export business was getting direct orders from the buyers abroad. However there were 'Indenting Agents' in

Cochin, working as representatives of buyers. They sell the "Purchase Orders' to the exporters. In fact Indenting Agents were making more money as their commission than actual exporters who invest money to make the consignment export worthy.

One "Mr. Chemmeen Varghese" was a big indenting Agent in Cochin (Chemmeen means Shrimp).He made money with shrimp business, hence the name. Till five years back, he was a retail fish merchant in Cochin fish market, and was living in a   shack in a slum. Somehow he got in contact with a Japanees Prawns and Shrimp buyer and became his agent. Now Chemmeen Varghese is living in a Mansion near sea shore, and lives like a duke.

Martin approached chemmeen Varghese for a trial order of one ton of shrimp.

" I know Martin, you are having money to start export business. I know you were making more money then as a licensed liquor Merchant." Varghese said with jealousy.

Martin ignored his comment ."My plan is to go for twenty to thirty tons per month if I get profitable orders." Martin said.

"If you have that much money to invest why don't you start a freezing plant.?" Varghese asked.

"Freezing plant? Oh. My god. It will cost twenty to twenty five lackhs of rupees I cannot dream of such a huge money." (Ten lakh is one million)

" Hay Martin, No industry ever came up in the world with own money of its entrepreneur.   The money is loan from financial institution-long term loan .Entrepreneur   has to invest only its margin money for the loan. Hardly ten percentage. That you now.   If you can start a freezing plant of your own, I will give you continuous orders without break." Chemmen Varghese assured him.

It was an encouraging information for Martin to start a freezing plant. He went to a State government Sponsored Financial Institution with his proposal of starting a freezing plant at Cochin.

"It is a very good idea. Very lucrative industry and very suitable for Cochi." The financial institution manager encouraged him. "Please put up your application for loan along with the project report." Manager suggested.

"Project Report? What is that.?" Martin wondered.

Manager explained what a project report was. "Project report is a written document, which provides all details on the overall picture of the proposed project. It contains detailed information about the land where the plant is constructed, details of the building of the proposed factory, manufacturing process, machinery details, raw materials, man power,marketing arrangements, financial analysis including re payment pattern etc. Project report gives a clear picture of the project."

"Who will make a project report for me. I don't know anything about it." Martin said.

"Not to worry about it. There is a consultant, a Chartered Accountant in the next building. His name is Raghu Ram Ayer. He is our auditor too. Go and meet him. Tell him that I have sent you" Manager suggested

Raghu Ram Ayer was an aged man of sixty.

"Mr. Martin, you first find out a suitable land to establish your factory. If the land is your own, it is easy to get the sanction and license from the Government. That proves the genuinness of the project.

Nowadays there are   may fictitious projects submitted to loot money from Government."

Martin was discussing the day to day progress of his project plan with Maggy. She suggested a suitable   land at Kannamaly, about ten kilometers South to Cochin.

" I think that is fifty cents of land with a thatched shed which belongs to my uncle Patrick. He was doing peeling contract work in that shed. Now he is not doing anything with that land. Just lying vacant. He is sick and in urgent need of some money to conduct the marriage of his daughter. He will be happy to sell the land to you." Maggi advised.

She took Martin to her uncle Patrick to discuss the deal. With her influence Martin could get the land at a cheaper rate. Within a few days the   sale deed of the property was registered in the name of "Martin Exports" , and that was the name Martin had proposed for his freezing plant.

The fifty cents of land was considered to be the initial capital expenditure and the project cost was thirty five lakhs of rupees. The term loan requirement was twenty lakhs rupees.

The project was approved by the financial institution. But another hurdle came up.

"What is collateral security? " The manager of financial institution asked Martin.

"Collateral security? What is that? "

"You must deposit a title deed of some other property valuing equal amount of the loan. The land purchased for the factory is already considered as a collateral security. But that is not sufficient. You must deposit another title deed to supplement the land value." The manager explained.

"I have two properties of my own. One is a two acres of land I had purchased in my mother's name at Mundalam pala. The Other one is at Fort Cochin and it is a two storied old building, in which we are living. It has got fifteen cents of land around it, as its enclosure. "

" Is it a concrete building? " The Manager asked.

"Oh. No. It is tile roofed. Very old building constructed about one hundred years back . It was a ' Mana' of a Kongini."

"Thats alright. Our surveyor will write in his report as a brand new, double storied concrete building, worth to cover your entire loan. You just pay him ten thousand rupees. " Manager smiled.

"Ten thousand rupees as bribe?"

"Don't use that word hereafter. Just say remuneration Or gift. Some how you want the job to be done. Don't you.?"

Martin agreed.

" One more thing." The manager said.

"Now what sir?

" The loan as per this project report is twenty lakhs rupees. I will make it as twenty lakhs twenty thousand rupees. The added twenty thousand is for me. When the loan is disbursed, you have to pay that amount to me. Understand? "

Martin was shocked. He looked at the cool face of the officer in bewilderment and hate .

"Sir. I have to pay back the amount. It is only a loan." Martin said.

" Hey Mister, you have to pay back the term loan within ten years in one,hundred and twenty monthly installments, with a moratorium of two years. The repayment would be a peanut for you if you run the business well"

"Yes of course, still I have to pay back.?"

" I will teach you later how to evade the repayments. For that you may have to give me another gift. That we will discuss later. Now let us proceed with this project. "

When Martin left the office with the acceptance letter of his project, he was not at all happy. His mind was boiling with grudge on the government officials. " vultures who loot the government money,

He understood why Kerala state is not developing developed in industrialization when compared to other States   Kerala will never improve until and unless its officials are made corruption free.

CHAPTER 28

THE TRAP

"Marty, there is an outstanding payment of three thousand rupees due from 'Lake Lord Leisure Hotel." Sobha told Martin when they were about to close that day's business.

They were in their Mattanchery office near boat jetty. Hamza also was present in the office. Though Martin had stopped his Chandlar supply   and allied business, Hamza continued to stick to Martin as his driver and aide.

The time was nearing dusk. 'Lake Lord Leisure' hotel was one of the famous star hotels in Cochin, situated near Thevara, with an upfront of back waters.Name of the hotel was written as "3L' as an abbreviation of 'Lake Lord Leisure'. Generally said as ' Thrill hotel': The hotel was owned by one Mr. Johar Singh, a Sardar from Punjab stationed in Dubai. He seldom visited the hotel. The hotel was   managed by one Mr. Augustine from Thiruvalla. He was a shrude and ruthless man but well educated, and specialized in hotel management. He was using all unethical means to make profit. He was running a most modern bar in the hotel serving all types of spirits available in the world, and Martin was one of his liquor suppliers. Drugs also were sold in the bar, though very secretly. The main customers were rich marine people. Sailors and ship crew from Merchant Navy were very lavish in spending money for pleasure and amusements, and Thrill hotel was their apt choice.

A luxury brothel house also was there in 'Thril' at the 'fifth floor' of the hotel. Mr. Augustin had employed well paid brokers to canvas and allure college girls and young hospital staff, by various means and bring to hotel. Getting in love with girls was one of their means. When a new 'recruit' overcame the initial delicacy and dilemma, they would become the " hot hosts" at the 'fifth floor"
Sabu, son of Kesavan Unni from Edacochin was one of such brokers of Thrill .

"Why haven't they paid our three thousand rupees so far? " Martin asked.

"I sent Abu our peon, several times for the money. Twice I talked to them over phone. Their Manager, one Mr.Augustin told me today until we give them further supply they won't pay the arrears." Sobha told.

"That is very unfair. I think it is better we handle this case directly."
Martin said, looking at Hamza.

"Sure sir, we will make his mama to pay the money cash down. Come on sir, " Hamza was ready for a confrontation and got up from his seat.

Darkness engulfed the world. But Willington Island was seen glowing with millions of lights. All the ships berthed at the wharf were well illuminated and presented a Diwaly show. Cochin was beautiful when all lights were on . All the streets were crowded as usual.

Hamza drove the car. Martin and Sobha were seated at rear. Whenever Martin drove she sat in front seat.

Sobha was droped at Mana. Hamza and Martin continued to drive towards hotel Thrill.

"It is his professional tactic to keep the payment in arrears to get further supply. He is a very tricky man indeed."Martin said.

"Don't worry sir, to day we will end up all his dirty tactics." Hamza murmured.

The hotel lobby was crowded with foreigners from a cruise ship. Martin followed by Hamza went to the reception counter and asked for

Manager. Usually the Manager Augustin used to sit in his glass cabin. On that day he was not seen in the cabin.

"May I help you Martin Sir," The lady at the counter asked him with a broad smile.

"Mary, where is Augustine? " Martin asked.

"What is the matter sir?"

"He owes me some money ; and due for long."

Mary picked up the phone to talk to someone. Hamza pushed down the button of the phone and said in a harsh voice."Tell us, where he is. We will meet him personally."

Mary looked at Hamza with fright in her beautiful eyes. A man who was writing on a thick register at the counter looked up. When saw Hamza, suddenly he got up to his feet.

'Sir, he is in banquet hall ." He said

"Why ? Has he also started dancing there?" Hamza asked with scorn in his voice .

Cabaret dances were performed in the banquet hall.

"No sir, today we have a special dance programe for our special guests. Bharath Natyam.! Owner of a Philipine Ship is our chief guest today.

He and his crew stay in this hotel tonight. Today's programe is only for them. Mr.Augustine is with them in the banquet hall." The man explained.

Martin and Hamza left the counter and walked toward elevator.

Hamza saw a bearded man sitting on a corner sofa in the lobby. He was looking down and reading a magazine. Hamza recognized him. He was Sabu, the son of Kesavan Unni. !

" Martin Sir, look   at the far end corner, who sits there?."   He said in whisper.

Martin saw him.

"Hay, what is that fellow is doing here?"   He asked in astonishment.

"Might have come to meet someone."

They ignored Sabu and , got into the elevator. There were not much people in the banquet hall. Hardly twenty people, and all of them were white skinned Philippinos. Augustine, a lofty man, in full suite, was talking to them.

At the far end of the hall there was a small stage with illuminated lights which indicated a stage show has just ended. By the side of the stage a band party was winding up their settings after their performance.

Augustin saw Martin and Hamza standing at the entrance of banquet hall. Hurriedly he went to them and greeted with a wide salesman's smile.

"Augustine sir, please don't play tricks with us. If we start paly tricks on you, up on God, I will tell you, you would never be able to bear with it." Hamza said in an unfriendly tone.

Augustine immediately recognized the danger. He got the message very clearly.

" Hamza Moopen, who am I to play tricks with you. You are the master of all tricks." He laughed very cordially.

"If you are sure of that, why the hell you evaded our payment?." Hamza raised his voice, in an unfriendly tone.

"For heavens sake, please calm down and talk slowly. Those guests sitting there are very important for us. You will be paid immediately. Please collect it from the counter, down." Augustin pleaded, by guiding them out of the hall.

Hamza pushed away his hand from his shoulder and said." I will go away by my own. Please don't try to push me out."

" I am sorry. I am not pushing you out." Augustin said

"Why Augustine, usually this hall was always found to be house full .

Today hardly a few. Why?" Martin asked to change the subject.

"Martin Sir, I told you, they are very special guests for us and they

booked the whole hall for today's special programme!"

"What special programme.? Full nude show!? "

"Oh. No. Today was a Bharath Nattiyam, Kerala special. And we have

got a super star, a pure virgin beauty. A   medical student." He said

proudly.

"Medical Student? To dance in this hotel?"

"Yes…Yes.. A medical student. After a great struggle our broker Sabu

brought her to this outfit . She is really a beautiful stuff. She will be

our asset."

"Augustin, you started to trap medical students also? It is too bad. Why

do you want to spoil their career.? " Hamza asked, sarcastically.

Suddenly Martin had an apprehension!"That beard man Sabu brought

that girl?" He asked.

"Yes..Yes.. you know him? Very smart fellow. He canvases girls for

us."

"Who is that medical girl he brought.?"

"Her name is Prabha. A Second year student from Alleppy Medical College. Very nice piece. Nicest of all here."

A jolting shiver pierced through the nerves of Martin. He looked at Hamza. He was also stunned by the information.

With a leap Martin caught hold of the tie of Augustin, dragged him very close to him and snarled with gritted teeth. "Do you know who that girl is?. She is my sister in law."

Augustin was shocked. But he said cooly. "She is only your sister – in – law. not your sister, is not? "

He wanted to say something further, But could not. Before that Martin's, fiet fell on his forehead like a steel hammer.

Augustine's eyes became blurred. A severe pain nailed on his brain. He received his second blow from Hamza with the edge of his palm, which was harder than a spade edge. Augustine fell down with a loud cry.

All in the banquet hall were shocked and stunned. They stood freezed looking at the fierce faces of Martin and Hamza.

Three Men in waiter's white uniforms came running. They were about to charge on Martin. Hamza drawn a sharp blade from underneath his shirt and roared at them. "If anyone dares to step one foot forward, I will slice his throat."

None moved forward. They stood still and looked at Hamza frightend.

Martin caught hold of the collar of one of them and asked. "Where is she?"

"Who?" He was shivering.

"The dancer girl. Prabha."

"I don't know sir."

One kick on his ribs made him to cry aloud." She is in third floor sir. Room NumberThree one three. One floor down. The chief guest's room. "

Martin ran out of banquet hall, closely followed by Hamza. The elevator was closed. They ran down the stairs and reached third floor . They saw the room 313. It was closed.

The corridor in third floor was in dark, seems none was in other rooms in that floor.

Hamza knocked the door of room 313.

There was no reply.

Martin knocked violently, yet there was no response.

Both the bulky men charged on the wooden door with their shoulders. With a violent cracking sound the door detached from its hinges and fell forward.

The sight inside was shocking!. A white skinned sizable man with big potbelly was standing near Prabha. He was wearing only a loin cloth. Prabha was in her dance costume frightened and terrified. Her blouse was torn and hair was disheveled. Her lips were bruised and stains of blood were seen. She had been tussled with and her dress was in disorder.

"What is this? Who the hell are you? What do you want?" The white skinned man asked in panic.

To his surprise Hamza caught hold of that man from back by his neck and thigh and lifted him over to his head for a 'sacrum hit'. The man riggled in the air and cried aloud like a wild swine.

"Hamza!" Martin shouted loudly .

"Don't Sacrum hit him. He is a foreigner and owner of a ship. If he dies we all would be locked up. Put him down. Put him down. You catch that man Sabu sitting down. He is the culprit. "

Hamza threw the man on to the bed . The man roared frantically.

"Shut up you white skinned pig. " Hamza lifted his leg and kicked him on his ribs.

"Don't kill me… Don't kill me…" he cried

"Prabha ran to Martin and knelt before him. She caught hold of his leg and cried. "Forgive me….Anna.. For give me… I was deceived. I was deceived.

∎∎

CHAPTER 29

CITY CLEARED

The well decorated and luxurious lobby of ' Lake Lord Lisure ' hotel was crowded with sailors and foreign tourists from a newly arrived Cruise Ship. Hotel had trained brokers posted at airport and wharf to canvas and bring customers to hotel.

Martin found it difficult to pass through the crowded, when he came out of elevator with Prabha. He had noticed that the corner Sofa, in which Sabu was sitting was occupied by European Couple. Sabu had gone!

Martin guided Prabha to his car, which was parked at the court yard of the hotel. When he drove the car out of hotel, with Prabha in front seat, he had seen Hamza was walking   by the side of the road with Sabu towards the deserted beach road. Hamza's hand was on Sabu's shoulder   and both were laughing on some joke. He noticed the overcast sky was preparing for a heavy rain. The lightning waves were wriggling through the clusters of dark clouds.

Prabhha was crying continuously with her head resting on the dash board. She was in utter desperation and upset. With great difficulty

Martin made her to talk on what had happened. She narrated the whole story with wimpering and crying intermittently.

She was in deep love with Sabu. He had promised to marry her immediately on getting a good job for him. He was without a good job, and was engaged in temple activities. But he was very optimistic of getting a good job as he was a graduate.

On that day Sabu reached Medical College in the morning. She was called out of the class. He was in a joyous mood. When asked he explained, and his explanation made Prabha also thrilled. He said he got a chance to act in a film being produced by 'Udaya Studio.' The famous stars Sathyan and Sheela were acting as hero and heroine. Sabu had to act in ten scenes. Remuneration would be very high. Complete shooting would be in and around Alleppey only, so that Prabha need not miss any class, He said.

" Why should I miss my class for you to attend   the film shooting " She asked.

"Oh, due to over excitement I forgot to tell you. I should have told you that first. You also would be acting in this cinema along with me. You have to dance with Sheela, the heroin." He said.

"Me… acting with Sheela?!" She was overwhelmed with excitement .

"The director wanted a female dancer to dance with the heroin . There would be three dances, I have suggested your name.   When I told them you had won the Kalathilakam Medal, immediately they agreed to take you in the   film. They   are scheduling the shooting of your scenes on Sundays so that you won't miss your class. " He explained.

Prabha was mesmarized by the information. She considered it as a great luck. Her mind was flying high to an unknown world. With lot of money, luxury and fame, and people would adore her, she dreamed.

"They have arranged an immediate interview with you. They want to see your performance. A special stage is also set up for you in a hotel at Cochin."He said

" In Cochin? " Prabha was astonished

"Yes. Hotel Lake Lord Lavish.!! "

"That is a star hotel, where Cabaret is staged."

"All Star hotels would have Cabaret. Why do we worry?"

"I have to talk to Annan and Chechi."

"Don't be a fool. Do you think they would agree if you ask their permission.?If you ask them they would never allow you. They will say that you would loose your studies. Your chechi would get jealous of you . She is also a dancer isn't she? ?. It would be quite natural."

"When is the interview?" She asked.

"Today evening"

Prabha believed his words

"Today at seven in the evening, . I will come at Four O clock to pick you up. Get ready with your costumes and anklets. Hotel will provide a taxi car to pick you. I will drop you back, before ten at night. Of course you will have a dinner with VIP's " He laughed.

As he said, she was taken to hotel at 6 PM

"He deceived me…deceived me. He was a cheat…I am a fool…fool" she cried hysterically….

Sabu! What a rascal he was?   How many girls might have been deceived by him Martin thought with utter hatred.

They reached Mana.

When Prabha appeared unexpectedly with Martin at night, Sobha was surprised. She got frightened when saw the torn blows and disordered dress.

" What happened to her? " Sobha panicked.

Before Martin could say anything Prabha knelt down in front of her Chechi, caught hold of her feet and cried aloud.

"Forgive me Chechi.. Forgive me… I had done a grave blunder. Forgive me…" She whimpered.

She caught hold of her and lifted her like a child. She made her to sit closer to her on the sofa.

When Martin explained what had happened, Sobha became wild and she lost her mind, she beat Prabha very violently. Then she embraced her sister and cried along with her, louder.

Martin's eyes also became moistured when saw both of them were crying together, embraced.

It was a dreadful night at Mana. None had any food, though it was made ready and served on the table. The lights were not put off. Martin lay awake on a Sofa in the drawing room. Sobha lay down on the cot with her sister, holding her arms like a child.

After midnight Prabha started shivering. Sobha got frightened. When checked Prabha had very high fever. The temperature was hundred and five when measured with thermometer. Prabha was gnashing her teeth and murmuring something unconsciously, in sleep.

She was rushed to the hospital.

Doctor gave her an intravenous injection and placed an ice bag on her head. She was admitted and administered drips.

"Let her be here for two three days. She is likely to get infected with pneumonia. I have to observe her." Doctor said to Martin

After two days a report appeared in all newspapers about "a hit and run" case. That happened two days before at Beach Road of Cochin. The ill fated victim was killed with broken hip bones and bruice on the spinal cord. The victim, was a young man with beard, was thrown off the road as the hit was very violent, probably by a high speed truck. The Police identified the victim as Sabu, son of Kesavan Unni, Mannath house, Edacochin. Police registered a case and started investigation!

Next day by eleven in the morning, Hamza went to 'Lake Lord Lisure hotel alone on his bullet motor bike. He went straight to the reception counter.

The lobby was free of rush and there was no customer to check in or out. The receptionist was talking over phone. Two sweepers were engaged in their works, and a uniformed attender was de-dusting sofas with a vacuum cleaner. All of them recoganised Hamza and greeted him with respect.

The Manager Augustin was sitting in his cabin just behind the reception counter. He was wearing a colour belt and a bandage was fixed on his brow. A mark of a bruise was visible on his chin.

"Hi, Madam, what happened to your Manager. He is sitting there with lot of decorations on his head." Hamza asked with a sarcastic smile.

"He slipped and fell on the stairs. " The receptionist said.

Hamza understood that the news of assault was not leaked out. Rather the hotel management was keeping the incident as a secret!

When Hamza opened the Cabin door, Augustin who was writing something on a book looked up and got up from his seat abruptly, with a jolt A great fear reflected on his eyes. He started shivering.

"Augustin, brother, please sit down, let us have some small chat. " Hamza was cool, and sat on a chair.

His sound sent a chill wave through the spines of Augustin. He sat down reluctantly and pleaded with fear. "Hamza Moopen, please don't beat me. "

"Beating you? By me ? Never."Hamza smiled" I have come to collect my money. The arrears due on bottles sold to you. Three thousand rupees".

" I will pay you now." He said

"That is not enough. Will have to compensate to the loss of honour of our sister Prabha How much do you value for the honour of a woman.?" Hamza asked.

"How much do you want.?"

"Now you pay fifty thousand rupees. Rest I will take from you when in need."

"Fifty thousand? " Augustin's eyes were widened .

"That is for the time being."

Augustin opened his drawer and took out bundles of notes and gave to him. He wraped the bundles in a news paper that was kept on the table.

"Do you know, what actually happened to Sabu? your Agent?" Hamza asked with cruel smile on his face.

"I know."

"Let that not happen to you."

"I will obey whatever you say, Hamza Moopen. Don't kill me. "

Augustin was at the verge of crying.

"Stop hosting the guests with girls." That was an order of the mafia king.

"Already stopped." Augustin said obediently.

"Dispose off all the girls you are keeping on the fifth floor. " That was another order.

"We had ten girls. We sent them all yesterday. "

"Let them not come here again in Cochin.

"No, Never."

"Stop Cabaret show."

"Already stopped. Now onwords only band and music."

CHAPTER 30

MARSO INTERNATINAL LTD

Maggy had played a vital role in Martins life. Her involvement had a great influence in his reformation. She guided him to an industrial sphere and made him an industrialist.

Maggy compelled Martin to stop the smuggled Liquor trade which he was doing under the cover of 'Chandlar business.

Though the plan to start a freezing plant by Martin was proposed by "Chemmeen Varghese, It was proceeded due to Maggy's compulsion. She supported him in each and every stage of the project implementation. Martin could purchase a suitable land for the construction of freezing plant at Kannamaly through her. She acted as his agent to negotiate the price of the land with her uncle. She went along with him to meet the government officials, financial institution, Industries Department, Electricity Board, Central excise and Sales Tax office to get the required papers approved.

Being an Anglo Indian, good looking and fluent in English speaking and a smart lady, she could persuade the officials very easily. She could get the papers through without getting into the hitch of redtapism.

Within fourteen months Martin could complete the freezing Plant project.

Chemmeen Varghese had kept up his word. He issued a standing purchase order for two tons of "white leg shrimps" to be shipped every fortnight to his principal company in Japan.

Martin became a registered exporter. But he was sad as thirty percentage of profit was parted as commission to Chemmeen Varghese .

"Until we get direct orders from the buyer, freezing plant project would never become lucrative." Martin said to Maggi.

"God brought you up to this level. He will guide you further. But whatever you are supposed to do, you must do it without hesitation. Whenever you disincline from the righteousness, God will withdraw his support and providence." She advised.

"I have not disinclined from righteousness so far."

"You did." Maggysaid strongly.

"What ? You name it.?

"You are avoiding to marry Sobha? You are doing injustice to her. She is a nice girl. She would be cursing you in her heart."

Martin never expected such a blunt comment from Maggy. That night Martin asked Sobha. "Do you want me to marry you?"

"That is my right." She replied, and her reply was firm.

" Even if I do not marry you officially, you are already my wife, and I love you."

"That is different. Wedding officially in public is my legitimate right. " She said.

Martin requested Michael and Maggy to organize his wedding

Maggy got Sobha to baptizedd, in Fort Cochin Church. Maritin married Sobha   in Mundalam Church without any pomp and show, in presence of very few close relatives and friends.

Mr. Chellppan, peon of Bronton Company brought a thick envelope, an aerogramme,   and gave it to Martin in his Mattanchery office. Chellappan was a very senior staff member of Bronton Company and he was very helpful to Martin when he was working there three years ago.

Though Martin's freezing plant was situated in Kannamaly village about   ten kilometers south to Cochin, he continued to function   his

Mattanchery office, for the operational advantages, as the wharf and customs office were close by.

The aerograme brought by Chellappan was a letter from his friend Ouseph , the seminarian in Vatican.

"This envelop was lying in our letter box for some time unclaimed. I happened to look at its address accidently, and found that it was for you, Thought of delivering it to you here. Hope you won't mind to give me a good tip, a very good one." He said with a smile.

Martin give him a one hundred rupee note. Chellappan was very happy. He did not expect that much.

"I know Martin sir, you are prosperous. May God bless you with further progress." Chellappan blessed him and left happily.

Martin looked at the heavy envelope . His friend might have ordained and become a priest, he thought. But, when he saw the Emirate's stamp and the from address he was astonished. The letter was posted from Dubai.!.Not from Vatican.

He slit opened the envelope. A colour photo was enclosed along with a few sheets of hand written letter.

When he saw at the photo Martin could not believe his eyes. He was shocked.

It was a group photo and Ouseph was standing along with a European family. He seemed to be fat. His pitch dark colour had faded a little. His right hand was circled on the waist of a beautiful white tall lady with blue eyes and cropped blond hair. She was holding a child with coloured skin. An elderly tall man and aged woman, apparently the parents of the European girl were standing behind the couples. All were in a very joyous mood with wide smile.

My God! It was unbelievable! Martin was astounded. His eyes became widened in disbelief.

The man who went to Vatican and was undergoing seminary training to become a priest is now standing embraced with a beautiful girl! The child, held by her was originated from him for sure. The eyes and face of the infant were very identical to Ouseph's. The skin of the child was coloured to confirm its parentage!

Martin sat back on his chair and started to read the letter with interest and curiosity.

The letter was written on an official letter head of "Osario Traders."

"From the desk of Managing Partner P.P. Ouseph." was printed on the top.

One full page was utilized to explain about the company "Osario Traders" and its business activities. The company possessed one milk blending plant ; twenty distribution outlets in the city of Dubai , twenty trucks, and about one hundred employees!

Two pages were narration of his life story. His seminary life. Homeopathy study, entangling in love affairs with Catherine etc.

It was like reading a thrilling novel when Martin read about the dismissal from Seminary, his escape from furious Georgeo natives and reaching in Dubai with his wife.

Ouseph wrote." Catherine is helping me in running the business. Almost all the employees are from Kerala. They are all very hard working type and very sincere. Unlike in Kerala, where they are said to be led by the trade union activists, here in Dubai, workers are being paid against their work done and not against the days they were present. As such they are to work."

When Martin read the last pages he became alert.

"Now my business in Dubai is in real problem. I may have to wind up the business if some alternative line is not found   out . Our uncle Rancisy now settled in Rome advised us to close the business and go to Georgeo, Rome to assist him in the business of Georgeo commune; which I am not interested. I want to stay in Dubai for which I want your support.

The UAE Government is   setting up Dairy farms in the outskirts of Dubai .Thousands of high breed cows were imported from Australia. Ship loads of strows and other cattle feeds also were imported. Within short time "Emirates Milk" will be   available throughout the   country and our blended milk the "Osario Milk" will be wiped out from the market. That means, our business would be closed for ever, and one hundred of our natives, the Keralites will loose their jobs

I have found out some other commodities which could be sold out through our Milk Distribution outlets. They are 'Mathy' and 'Kappa' (means Sardine fish and raw tapioca)

As you know 'Mathy curry' and ' Kappa are the favourate dishes of Keralites. In Dubai and Abudhabi alone there are about three hundred thousand Keralits living. If we consider the whole of UAE it would be more than   three million and they all will buy Kappa and Mathy if they are made available in the market.

In Dubai we will get all types of fishes except Mathy as they are not seen in Sea of Gulf.

"Will it be possible for you to send one tone of mathy and one tone of Kappa if we place a trial order to evaluate the market.?" Ouseph asked in his letter.

"Martin found a new scope of export business without a middle man or a commission agent!

Mathy and Kappa were two low cost commodities available in Kerala market. Mathy was costing only ten paisa per kilo. Fresh Kappa was costing twenty paisa per kilo and both the items were available in plenty in Kerala. No one would think of exporting such low value and negligible items.

Martin booked an overseas call to Dubai on the number printed on the letter head of ' Osario Traders.' He had to wait anxiously about half an hour to get the call through. It was the first time Martin was making an overseas call.

The friends were talking to each other after a period of eight years! Yet both of them were very familiar to their voices. They talked for about fifteen minutes about their personal lives.

"Now let us talk about the export of Mathy and Kappa." Martin said.

"I found a big scope for both in gulf market. I have made a statistical survey about it through an agency. The result is very encouraging. I think we will make a try. I will send you a formal order for one tone each for both the items. Work out at what rate you would be able to send the consignment. I will send you the money by letter of credit along with order." Ouseph said.

"Borh the items are very cheap in the market if we buy a smaller quantity for the kitchen use. When go for bulk purchase, the procurement expenditure would be high. We must have collection centres, transporting, labour cost all things would be added up. Then comes to processing, packing, freezing. All that would be expensive ." Martin explained the practical difficulties.

" I understand. Just work out and let me know the cost."

" I am exporting frozen shrimps to Japan with thirty percentage margin. Out of the profit I am compelled to pay thirty percentage as Agency commission." Martin said.

" You work out Martin. The local vendors are to meet all these expenditures to bring the items to market for sale and they make profit. So, it would be possible."

"Ok… Let me try."

"You work out with fifty percentage margin for you after meeting all the expenditure. I want the FOB price." (Freight on board)

"OK. I will call you within three days."

They hung up.

After a detailed market survey and costing, Martin confirmed his price for Mathy as Rs. Twenty per kilo and Rs.thirty per kilo for Kappa, Both with hundred percentage margins.

Cleaned frozen Mathy, packed in one kilo multi colour printed waxed packets and ten such packets are packed in a master carton.   One hundred cartons would weigh one ton. Cleaned fresh Kappa was packed in bamboo baskets, at ten kilo per each basket.

The first consignment of ' Kappa' and Mathi exported from Cochin Port was on 20th August 1968 by "Martin exporters Cochin", consigned to " Osario Trades Dubai." And it was a record.

It was a start; and it was successful. Within one month Martin received order for ten tons of Mathy and Kappa each and later it was increased to one container of both the items every week

Martin had to expand his procuring network for Mathy, through the entire costal area from Kanyakumari to Mangalore with hundreds of agents in the field. He also had to widen his Kappa collecting network throughout eastern ghatt region.

Ousesph had established his sales net work , in all UAE emirates, through agents.

A new company was registered at Cochin named " Marso International " in which Martin Exporters of Cochin and Osario Traders of Dubai were partners and equal share holders. The company became a multi crore project within five years.

The trade relation between Martin Manassery and Ouseph, Palliparambil son of Pathrose the grave digger had its root sprouted about nine years back when they were studying in Pala, St. Thomas

School, in the exchange of a portion of Dosa against a piece of boiled

Kappa.

****